StringNet

教你使用英文同義字(II)

李路得●著

英語辭彙不NG

本書介紹

線上語料庫是甚麼？

英語線上語料庫（corpus）是新興的英語學習工具。傳統字典的例句及教科書的文章大多是為教學而刻意寫作，常被質疑和英美人士實際使用的英文不盡相同，英語線上語料庫則是蒐集真實語料如英美國家的報章雜誌，將其中的單字或片語加以整理彙編，透過網路提供使用者在線上搜尋某一個單字或片語出現的所有句子。目前世界各種語言有許多已經建立其語料庫，英語最大的語料庫則是BNC（British National Corpus）語料庫，內容涵蓋英美國家的報章雜誌、學術論文、小說、廣播節目等真實語料，蒐集單字量超過一億。英語學習者可以藉由語料庫查詢單字及片語上下文及其前後出現的搭配詞，以了解精準意義及用法，以此方式能夠學習真實世界的英語用法，特別在英文寫作的遣詞用字上有明顯裨益。

StringNet是甚麼？

在BNC語料庫（http://www.natcorp.ox.ac.uk/）中，英文單字與片語只有經過簡單初步的彙整，後來拜科技之賜，有一些學者把BNC的內容作進一步詳細的分類，能夠查詢更多資訊，本書採用的StringNet（http://www.lexchecker.org/index.php）是國立中央大學特聘研究講座David Wible教授主持創立的多功能英語線上語料庫查詢系統，內容以BNC（British National Corpus）語料庫為主，整理其中單字及片語，計算某個單字在語料庫出現的次數，若該單字有二種詞類，亦分別計算列出，以recruit為例，它可以當動詞和名詞，其動詞出現1934次，名詞出現871次；也分析某單字常常和那些搭配詞一起使用，提供片語字串，如recruit from和recruit new members等；還可依搭配詞的詞類分別檢索，並顯示搭配詞在語料庫中出現的次數從最多到最少，如recruit當動詞時後面出現的複數名詞有staff（28次）、

people（21次）、members（13次）、student（9次）、workers（6次）、women（6次）等等，其中staff出現最多次，由此可知這二個字時常一起使用；除了顯示和常用搭配詞形成的字串以外，StringNet也提供包含某單字或片語的所有完整句子。

如何使用本書？

本書的目的在於釐清意義容易混淆的英文單字，編排時以中文意義為考量，而非英文單字的拼法，因此本書內容是按照中文注音符號的順序排列，已經出版第一冊包含ㄅ到ㄈ，本書為第二冊，包含ㄉ到ㄍ，後續內容待日後陸續編寫出版。

本書包含91組同義字，每一組的內容分為四部份：

1.語料庫出現次數

藉著比較各同義字在語料庫出現的次數多寡顯示各單字的常用程度，例如：

StringNet語料庫出現次數

flatter	insinuate	fawn
482 (v.)	92 (v.)	42 (v.)

在此表示動詞flatter在StringNet中的出現次數是482次，動詞insinuate出現92次，動詞fawn出現42次。

2.常用句型和例句

幫助讀者明白每個單字可以出現的句子結構以及例句，建立上下語文情境的概念，例如不及物動詞（vi.）後面不能出現受詞，或某些動詞常用在被動語態，例如：

S + flatter + O（+ about/ on + N）
S + be flattered + that 子句
S + flatter oneself that 子句

The employees were eager to **flatter** their boss at his birthday party.
His praise **flattered** her vanity, even though she didn’t like him at all.
She **flattered herself that** she was the most attractive girl at the party.

3.常用搭配詞

若要探討的單字是及物動詞，則提供該動詞前面常用的主詞和後面常用的受詞；若是不及物動詞，則提供該前面常用的主詞和後面常用的介系詞或副詞；若是形容詞，則提供後面常用的名詞；但是不一定全部都提供，會斟酌個別單字的使用情形。以動詞swing為例，常用的主詞如下：

(det.) n. + swing

door, arms, legs, pendulum hair, mood, wind, opinion, men, foot, tail, sign, boy, fish, gates, boat, hand.

在此(det.)表示可能出現限定詞a、the，所有格或量詞等，n. 表示下方所列的單字可出現在此位置，下方名詞從door到hand是依照在語料庫出現次數從多到少依序排列，也就是說door最常用作swing的主詞。在StringNet有完整句子，例如The front door swung open and Mrs Vigo came in, holding the child. (http://www.lexchecker.org/hyngram/hyngram_ex.php?hyngram_cjson=[30,%20287969]&meta_offset=105834492)

swing常用的受詞如下:

swing + (det.) n.

leg, axe, balance, door, club, pendulum gun, rod, bat, stick, gate, handle, scarf, hammer, basket, bag.

4.綜合整理

在此解釋同一組同義字個別單字的意義，並說明搭配詞的特性，以幫助讀者比較同義字之間意義與搭配詞的異同，在寫作時能選擇正確的單字及正確的搭配詞。全書最後並有單字索引，可以依照字母順序查考單字。

目 次

Unit 1 搭乘

StringNet語料庫出現次數

mount	embark	board
3079	1336	837

mount（vt.）

❖ 常用句型

S（人）+ mount + O（交通工具）

❖ 例句

He helped his son mount the horse.
他幫助兒子登上馬背。

❖ 常用搭配詞

mount +（det.）n.
horse, bike, camel.

embark（vi./vt.）

❖ 常用句型

S（人）+ embark on + O（交通工具）
S（交通工具）+ embark + O（人）

❖ 例句

They embarked on the cruise on July 3.
他們七月三日登上那郵輪。
The ferry stopped to embark passengers.
這渡輪停下來載客。

❖ 常用搭配詞

embark on +（det.）n.
cruise.

board（vi./vt.）

❖ 常用句型

S（人）+ board + O（交通工具）
S（交通工具）+ be boarding

❖ 例句

They boarded the train for Boston.
他們登上往波士頓的火車。
Your flight will be boarding in 30 minutes.
你的班機在30分鐘內可以登機。

❖ 常用搭配詞

board +（det.） n.
train, plane, coach, aircraft, ferry, chopper, flight, ship, bus.

綜合整理

mount	指騎上機車、腳踏車、動物等，相反詞為dismount。
embark	表示郵輪等交通工具開始讓旅客進入，相反詞為disembark，但是這個字主要意義大多指著手開始進行某事（embark on/ upon something）。
board	正式用字，指搭乘公車、飛機、貨船等大型交通工具，也指飛機等交通工具開始讓旅客進入。

Unit 2 達到，達成

StringNet語料庫出現次數

reach	achieve	attain	accomplish
22346	16688	1229	964

reach（vt.）

❖ 常用句型

S + reach + O

❖ 片語

reach a peak/climax
達到頂峰
reach the age of
達到某個年齡

❖ 常用搭配詞

reach +（det.）n.

end, stage, point, age, conclusion, top, door, final, summit, limit, office, place, pinnacle, level, decision, threshold, equilibrium, boundary, quota, rank, ceiling, proportion.

achieve（vi.）

❖ 常用句型

S + achieve + O

❖ 片語

achieve the aim/goal/objective
達到目標
achieve the desired result
達到希望的結果
achieve the desired weight goals
達到希望的體重目標

❖ 常用搭配詞

achieve +（det.）n.

objective, goal, end, aim, success, result, degree, target, status, measure, change, distinction, position, result, feat, balance, level, effect, purpose, improvement, victory, progress, independence, object, understanding, prominence, qualification, fairness, impact, continuity, ambition, equality, skill, pinnacle, standard, recognition, notoriety, condition, expansion, compromise, outcome, fame.

attain（vt.）

❖ 常用句型

S + attain + O

❖ 片語

attain one's ideal weight/ shape
達到某人的理想體重/身材

❖ 常用搭配詞

attain +（det.）n.
age, rank, status, standard, level, ridge, ideal, object, aim, domain.

attain the + n. of
rank, standard, status, degree, level, age.

accomplish（vt.）

❖ 常用句型

S + accomplish + O
S + be accomplished by/in/with/without + N

❖ 常用搭配詞

accomplish +（det.）n.

task, objective, journey, feat, transition, contact, move.

accomplish the n. + of

conversion, task, end, flexibility, reduction, detachment, reorganization.

綜合整理

reach	可指到達一段發展中的某個階段（如年齡等）、速度或數量的增加到某個程度、也可以指一群人成功達成意見的一致，以及伸手達到某個東西。
achieve	成功地完成某件事情或達到良好的結果，尤其是指經過努力。可當不及物動詞表示在工作上或活動上的成功。
attain	經過一段長時間努力後達到某個目標，尤其指某個水準、大小、或年齡等。
accomplish	成功地完成某件事情，基本意義和achieve相似，但也表示完成需要一段時間的工作，所以後面可接task, journey, the reduction of, the reorganization of 等表示一段過程的名詞，achieve則沒有此種用法。

Unit 3 打擊

StringNet語料庫出現次數

hit	beat	strike	blow	bat
10331	8024	7091	2257	426

hit（vt.）

❖ 常用句型

S + hit + something/ somebody（+ with something）

❖ 片語

hit someone in the face
掌摑
hit the headline
登上頭條新聞
hit the nail on the head
釘釘子

❖ 常用搭配詞

hit +（det.）n.

ball, ground, headlines, face, body, floor, post, target, wall, bar, roof, back, front, side, city, fan, car, surface, girl, forehead, wife, hand, opponent, tooth, shoulder.

beat（vt.）

❖ 常用句型

S + beat + O

❖ 例句

The slave was beaten to death.
這奴隸被活活打死。

❖ 常用搭配詞

be + adv. beaten

badly, severely, gradually, savagely, brutally, regularly, physically, repeatedly, lightly, wildly, violent, reportedly, allegedly, viciously.

strike（vt.）

❖ 常用句型

S + strike + O（+ prep. + N）

❖ 例句

He slipped, striking his head on the rock.
他滑一跤，頭撞到岩石。

The stone struck him on the back of the head.
石頭打到他的後腦勺。

❖ 常用搭配詞

strike +（det.） n.
note, chord, face, wall, visitor, blow, shot, Philippine.

（det.） n. + strike
thought, clock, disaster, lightning, tragedy, bullet, power, sun, light, accident, blow, shot, raider, killer, chance, wind, pain, plague.

blow（n.）

❖ 例句

He was killed by a blow on the head.
他的致命傷是頭部重擊。

❖ 常用搭配詞

v. + a blow
deal, suffer, strike, deliver, inflict, represent, give, render, avoid, receive, survive.

a + adj. + blow to
severe, heavy, serious, devastating, major, crushing, unfair, huge, fatal, cruel, double, mortal, mighty, critical, savage, shattering, overwhelming, crippling.

bat（vi./vt.）

❖ 例句

He batted for 149 minutes in the baseball game.
他在這場棒球賽中打擊149分鐘。

❖ 常用搭配詞

bat +（det.）n.
ball, car.

綜合整理

hit	用手或工具快速撞擊某物或某人，尤其是造成毀壞或疼痛。
beat	指重複持續的擊打，常用被動語態，另有打敗等其他意思。
strike	主要用在寫作文章，等於口語的hit，表示用力撞擊或掉落於某物的表面，另外也表示用手部或武器攻擊，屬於正式用字。
blow	這個字表示打擊的意思只用在名詞，指用手、工具、或武器用力擊打，但也常用來表示使某件事情挫敗而無法實行。另有轟炸等其他意思。
bat	用球棒或球拍擊打，常當作不及物動詞表示棒球運動的打擊。另指眨眼勾引（bat one's eyes）。

Unit 4 大意，大綱

StringNet語料庫出現次數

summary	outline	synopsis
2460	1936	96

summary（n.）

❖ 片語

a summary of the financial balances
財務結餘的摘要

❖ 常用搭配詞

summary of the + n.

result, information, finding, court, event, development, advice, rational, report, cost.

adj. + summary

brief, good, short, useful, fair, concise, full, overall, accessible, simple, four-minute, monthly, convenient, thorough, written, adequate, periodic, comprehensive, lengthy.

outline（n.）

❖ 片語

an outline of the major differences between A and B
A和B主要差異的大綱

❖ 常用搭配詞

adj. + outline
brief, broad, general, basic, rough, useful, historical, detailed, clear.

outline of the n.
way, theory, law, circumstance, concept, method, reason, history, principle, effect.

synopsis（n.）

❖ 片語

the synopsis of the film
這部電影的劇情大綱

❖ 常用搭配詞

adj. + synopsis
one-page, brief, schematic, initial, one-paragraph.

synopsis of the + n.
play, characteristics, cover, production, action, history, opportunity.

綜合整理

summary	泛指統括某件事情主要內容的短文，例如把一篇長文章的大意濃縮成一小段文字。
outline	除了指某件事情的主旨之外，也指將每一重點逐一分點分句，條列式的呈現，如論文大綱。
synopsis	常指書本、電影、戲劇等的劇情概要。也指對照表，一覽表。

Unit 5 擔憂的

StringNet語料庫出現次數

concerned	worried	anxious	upset	troubled
15492	3567	2941	1650	711

concerned（adj.）

❖ 常用句型

S + be concerned about/ for
S + be concerned + that 子句

❖ 例句

They are concerned about their mother's health.
他們很擔心母親的健康

❖ 常用搭配詞

be concerned about +（det.）n.

case, impact, content, arrangement, advert, aspect, danger, decline, safety, reputation, health, prospect, man, future, overcrowding, possibility, life, injury, situation, damage, everyone, loss, cost, result, oneself, ability, trend, lack, poverty, relative, horse, strain, stagnation.

worried（adj.）

❖ 常用句型

S + be worried about/ by
S + be worried + that 子句

❖ 例句

Don't be worried about money.
不要擔心錢的問題。

❖ 常用搭配詞

worried about +（det.）n.

problem, error, effect, outcome, provision, mood, son, drug, matter, bill, passports, strength, me, sermon, duration, way, inability, consequence, responsibility, business, him, instability, nothing, state, loss, age, arrangement, quality, tone, citizen, money, mole, result, surpluses, ownership, job, living standard, us, litter, technique, body, ability politics, plate, fork, thunderstorm.

worried + n.

parents, look, expression, man, glance, voice, people, eyes, faces, tone, mother, friends.

anxious（adj.）

❖ 常用句型

S + anxious about/ for + N
S + anxious + that 子句

❖ 例句

She was anxious about the result of the health examination.
她很擔憂健康檢查的結果。

❖ 常用搭配詞

anxious about +（det.） n.

children, standard, surplus, delay, attitude, war, journey, man, safety, tomorrow, situation, fate, lack, blood pressure, prospect, failure, life, precariousness, threat, risk, condition, obsession, result, demand, flight, weather, time, piracy, health, progress, side effect, anxiety, question, trip, change, possibility, surgery, traveling, consequence, outcome, whereabouts, future, implication, injury, state of mind, extent, porcelain, welfare, moral, impact, visit, collapse.

anxious + n.

moments, parent, face, eyes, wait, state, voice, expression, time, look, thoughts, glances, woman, people, hours, horses, person, questions, weeks, attention, personality, letters, silence.

upset（adj.）

❖ 常用句型

S + be upset about/ by/ at
S + be upset + that 子句

❖ 例句

Mr. White was upset that his application of the loan had been rejected.
懷特先生因為申請貸款被拒而煩惱憂慮。

❖ 常用搭配詞

upset about +（det.）n.

plan, something, anything, will, husband, resignation, incident, accident, idea, prospect, death, relationship, food, story, behavior, aspect, kid, illness, decision, appearance, baby, image, way, work, it.

upset + n.

stomach, people, tummy.

troubled（adj.）

❖ 常用句型

s + be/ look troubled by + N

❖ 例句

Are you all right？ You look troubled.
你還好嗎？你看起來心神不寧。

❖ 常用搭配詞

be troubled by +（det.） n.

doubt, question, problem, dream, difficulty, demon, feelings, prediction, conflict, unrest, conscience, thoughts, loss, issue, injury, demand, strike, contradiction, dream, anxiety, marriage, burden, blotch, moon, drum, suspicion, reporters, telephone call, detail, health, bombing, liaison, atmosphere, shoulder, asthma, ailment, itching, divorce, autograph-hunter, snipers.

troubled + n.

times, waters, face, eyes, marriage, soul, relationship, mind, people, children, expression, years, period.

綜合整理

concerned	擔心某件事情。about後面可以接事物或人作為受詞，但是通常是事情而比較少是人。
worried	擔心某人或某件事情未來的發展。about後面可以接事物或人作為受詞，但比其他單字後面常接人。worried後面若接名詞常表示充滿擔憂的人物或表情。
anxious	擔憂某件事情。後面若接名詞常表示充滿擔憂的時刻、人物、或表情。
upset	表示因為已經發生的壞事而不高興或擔憂。後面若接名詞常表示身體某部位不舒服（例如upset stomach）或不安的人。
troubled	troubled通常用在被動語態be troubled by，後面的受詞通常是事物，若是人的話表示深受其擾而感到心煩。後面若接名詞常表示擔憂的表情或人物，另外也表示充滿問題的（例如troubled times）。

Unit 6 淡化，使不重要

StringNet語料庫出現次數

downgrade	understate	downplay
169	153	36

downgrade（vt.）

❖ 常用句型

S + downgrade + O

❖ 例句

Apprenticeship system should not be downgraded.
學徒制度不應該被貶低。
We shouldn't downgrade the seriousness of violence
我們不應該小看暴力的嚴重性

❖ 常用搭配詞

downgrade +（det.）n.

role, commitment, forecast, status, study, possibility, seriousness, contribution, staff, individual, women, rating, importance, diplomatic relations with.

（det.）n. + downgrade

broker, analyst, judgment, assessment.

understate（vt.）

❖ 常用句型

S + understate + O

❖ 片語

to understate the pace of deterioration
少報惡化的速度
to understate the number of people unemployed
少報失業人口的數量

❖ 常用搭配詞

understate +（det.）n.
extent, influence, importance, value, case, price, depth, magnitude, scale.

（det.）n. + understate
migrant, assessment, statistics, figure, poll, company, record, estimator, company, comparison, data.

downplay（vt.）

❖ 常用句型

S + downplay + O

❖ 片語

to downplay the scale of the famine

把飢荒的規模輕描淡寫

to downplay one's importance

淡化某人的重要性

❖ 常用搭配詞

downplay +（det.）n.

importance, expectations, difference, scale, myth, value, effect, part, role.

（det.）n. + downplay

institution, Russia（country）, Whitney（person）.

綜合整理

downgrade	使某件事情看起來比較不重要或沒價值，常用於被動語態。屬於有意志行為，主詞通常是可以表達態度的人、機構、或報告資料等，受詞可以是人，表示輕視。
understate	只在言詞上將某事的嚴重性或重要性輕描淡寫，屬於有意志行為，主詞通常是可以表達言詞的人、機構、或報告資料等，受詞不可以是人。
downplay	使某件事情看起來比較不重要，受詞不可以是人。屬於有意志行為，主詞通常是可以表達態度的人、機構、或報告資料等，受詞不可以是人。

Unit 7 當作，視為

StringNet語料庫出現次數

see	consider	regard	view	reckon	deem
183800（v.）	28532	12900（v.）	4283（v.）	3878	1621

以上單字意思相近，後面受詞皆可以是人或非人，唯有受詞補語前的介系詞有的是as，有的是to be，有的二者皆可，整理如下：

單字	解釋	+ sb/sth + as	+ sb/sth to be
see	和view相似。	○	X
consider	強調個人意見。	X	○
regard	正式用字。	○	X
view	和see相似。	○	X
reckon	常用被動。	○	○
deem	正式用字，常用被動，和consider相似。	X	○

Unit 8 擋住，阻擋

StringNet語料庫出現次數

block	bar	obstruct	blockade	barricade
2571	918	409	96	60

block（vt.）

❖ 常用句型

S + block + O

❖ 例句

The rock was blocking the road.
這塊岩石把路堵住了。
The pillar next to their seat blocked their view of the stage.
他們座位旁邊的柱子擋住他們看舞台的視線。

❖ 常用搭配詞

block +（det.）n.

road, way, flow, entrance, release, path, pavement, action, passage, absortion, view, induction, track, street, route, doorway, city, development, exit, door, hole, sun, sunlight, drain.

bar（vt.）

❖ 常用句型

S + bar + O
S + be barred

❖ 例句

A locked gate barred the way.
一道上鎖的門擋住了去路。

bar +（det.）n.
body, right, return, passage, exit, sight, line, car.

（det.）n. + be barred
window, way, car, escape, journalist, lawyer, men, observer, reporter.

obstruct（vt.）

❖ 常用句型

S + obstruct + O

❖ 例句

The sign obstructed the driver's vision to the left.
這招牌擋住左轉駕駛人的視線。
He was charged with obstructing the police in execution of their duty.
他被控妨礙警察執行公務。

❖ 常用搭配詞

obstruct +（det.）n.
highway, passage, course, line, access, door, view, path.

blockade（vt.）

❖ 常用句型

S + blockade + O

❖ 例句

The radio broadcast news of students blockading the train station.
收音機新聞報導說學生封鎖火車站。

❖ 常用搭配詞

blockade +（det.）n.
island, road, dump, harbor, strait, train station, gulf, capital, door, entrance, vision, glare.

barricade（vt.）

❖ 常用句型

S + barricade + O

❖ 例句

The protesters barricaded themselves inside a castle.
這些抗議人士把自己關在一個城堡裡。

❖ 常用搭配詞

barricade +（det.）n.

oneself, building, gate, room, window, cell, path, legation, road.

綜合整理

block	擋在正前方、橫跨或在中央，可指擋住視線。另外也指阻擋某件事情的發生或發展。
bar	表示某物擋住去路，也指政府的限制令，使人不能出境或做某事，常用被動語態，尤其指窗戶被木條釘住而無法打開。
obstruct	和block相似，表示擋住道路或通道，也表示擋住某人的去路或視線。另外常用來表示妨礙警察執行公務（obstructing the police in execution of their duty）。
blockade	指封鎖整個區域阻擋人員、車輛或物資的進出，常見於示威抗爭或軍事行動。較常用作名詞表示封鎖。
barricade	較常當做名詞表示路障，當動詞表示以路障擋住。也表示為防衛起見把自己封鎖在一個地方不讓外人進入。

Unit 9 等候，等待

StringNet語料庫出現次數

expect	wait	look forward to	await
28016	19393	2254（BNC語料庫）	2001

expect（vt.）

❖ 常用句型

S + expect + O

❖ 例句

Please come in. He has been expecting you.
請進，他已經在等你。

❖ 常用搭配詞

expect + n.

Mr.（姓）, trouble, her third child, pupils, visitor, support, payment, information, result, change, word, risk.

wait（vi.）

❖ 常用句型

S + wait for + N

❖ 例句

The tourists were waiting for the skies to clear.
觀光客在等天氣放晴。
You can read a book while waiting for your flight.
你在等班機時可以看書。

❖ 常用搭配詞

wait for +（det.） n.
reply, bus, moment, train, response, return, reply, mother, money, kiss, taxi, decision, chance, year, flight, miracle, break, day, sign, telephone, report, signal.

look forward to（vt.）

❖ 常用句型

S + look forward to + N

❖ 例句

We were looking forward to gorging ourselves on an entire turkey.
我們期待好好大吃一整隻火雞。

❖ 常用搭配詞

look forward to + Ving

seeing, hearing, meeting, going, getting, working, having, receiving, welcoming, spending, doing, playing, reading, continuing, coming, starting, returning, telling, learning, making, moving, giving, enjoying, showing, putting, visiting, taking, leaving, trying, traveling, discussing, celebrating.

look forward to + one's n.

return, visit, time, future, arrival, day, trip, retirement, death, company, holiday, reply, appointment, lecture, honeymoon, breakfast.

await（vt.）

❖ 常用句型

S + await + O

❖ 例句

She was eagerly awaiting his invitation to the prom.
她熱切地等待他來邀她去舞會。

❖ 常用搭配詞

await +（det.） n.

trial, arrival, news, execution, sentence, discovery, turn, return, fate, confirmation, development, connection, shipment, approval, transfer, restoration, event, publication, him, you, us, instruction, order, clearance, decision, call, chance, opportunity, return, rescue, result, clarification, export, funding, processing, verdict, attention, summon, adoption.

綜合整理

expect	等待已經約好的人或安排好的事物或相信會發生的事情，是不及物動詞，後面必須接for等介系詞才能接受詞。
wait	甚麼事情都不做，只單純等待，直到某件事情發生或某人來到。
look forward to	指滿懷興奮地等待，盼望某事趕快發生，後面受詞通常是動名詞或所有格加名詞，受詞不多是人，多半是事情或時間。
await	意義和wait一樣，但await是及物動詞，可以接受詞。

Unit 10 瞪，凝視

StringNet語料庫出現次數

stare	gaze	gape	gawk
7526	2133	167	5（BNC語料庫）

stare（vi.）

❖ 常用句型

S + stare at + O

❖ 例句

Why are you staring at him like that？
你為何那樣盯著他？

❖ 常用搭配詞

stare at 人 in + n.
disbelief, horror, astonishment, silence, shock, surprise, amazement, bewilderment, confusion, dismay, exasperation, perplexity, terror, despair.

stare at +（det.）n.
him, her, ceiling, floor, wall, ground, man, screen, sky, picture, door, window, table, fire, carpet, paper, sea, water, it, house, phone, woman, boy.

stare + adv.

down, out, up, back, straight, blankly, ahead, hard, fixedly, intently, across, blindly, unseeingly, around, in, round, upward, moodily, right, vacantly, over, wildly, bleakly, coldly, directly, stonily, coolly, angrily, thoughtfully, dully, suspiciously, silently, impassively, glumly, sadly, gloomily, incredulously, morosely, grimly, unblinkingly, dazedly, apprehensively, fiercely, rigidly.

gaze（vi.）

❖ 常用句型

S + gaze into/ at + N

❖ 片語

to gaze out of the window
凝視窗外

to gaze into space
茫然看著前方

❖ 常用搭配詞

gaze at 人 in + n.

silence, astonishment, dismay, disbelief, admiration, fascination, confusion, alarm, mystification, bliss, innocence, surprise, amazement, horror.

gaze at +（det.）n.

him, it, her, me, ceiling, camera, Madonna, table, breakfast, ground.

gaze + adv. at

up, down, back, out, across, thoughtfully, fixedly, intently, longingly, about, directly, admiringly, helplessly, abstractedly, lovingly, hard, unseeingly, straight, absently, heavily, earnestly, around, petulantly, round, calmly, dumbly, expressionlessly, steadily, appealingly, wistfully, dreamily, gloomily, upwards.

gape（vi.）

❖ 常用句型

S + gape at + N

❖ 例句

Shocked, she gaped at him.
她嚇得目瞪口呆地看著他。

❖ 常用搭配詞

gape at +（det.） n.

him, her, me, it, room, cup, screen, damage, glass.

gape + adv.

up, down, back, once, briefly, numbly, stupidly, fully, blankly, unattractively.

gawk（vi.）

❖ 常用句型

S + gawk at + N

❖ 例句

Don't gawk at the prince.
別痴痴地看著王子。

❖ 常用搭配詞

gawk at +（det.）n.
people, machine, platform, him.

gawk in + n.
wonder, surprise.

綜合整理

gaze	不自覺地盯著某人或某物看很久。
stare	強調因為驚訝、生氣、或無聊而一直盯著某人或某物。
gape	強調因為震驚而張口結舌，目瞪口呆地一直盯著某人或某物。
gawk	指傻傻地一直看著。

Unit 11 滴下

StringNet語料庫出現次數

drop	drip	dribble
10232	649	192

drop（n.）

❖ 片語

a few drops of rain
幾滴雨
icy drops of water
幾滴冰水

❖ 常用搭配詞

a drop of + n.
water, rain, blood, wine, lavender, oil, milk, alcohol, acid, sweat, whisky, ink, liquid, moisture, lemonade, tea.

drip（vi.）

❖ 常用句型

S + drip（+ adv./ prep. + N）

❖ 例句

His sweat dripped down his neck.
他的汗從他的脖子滴下來。

The tap in the bathroom is dripping.
浴室的水龍頭在滴水。

❖ 常用搭配詞

（det.）n. + drip

water, blood, rain, tap, sweat, hair, wax, saliva, moisture, mouth, liquid.

dribble（vi. / vt.）

❖ 常用句型

S + dribble（+ prep. + N）
S + dribble + O

❖ 例句

She sat alone watching the rainwater dribbling down the window.
她獨自坐著，一邊看著雨水從窗戶滴落下來。

She dribbled a few drops of oil over the salad.
她滴幾滴橄欖油在沙拉上。

❖ 常用搭配詞

（det.）n. + dribble

blood, saliva, mouth, milk, fluid.

❖ 綜合整理

drop	表示和水滴有關的意義時通常是名詞，表示液體的一滴。
drip	是不及物動詞，主詞可以是液體滴下的源頭如頭髮或水龍頭等，也可以是液體本身。
dribble	指液體緩慢流出在某表面上，形成不規則的細流，如皮膚上流血。當不及物動詞時的主詞是液體本身；當及物動詞時表示使液體滴下，主詞是人，也是主事者。

Unit 12 敵人，對手

StringNet語料庫出現次數

enemy	opponent	rival	competitor	foe
4539	3039	2404	2214	491

challenger	contender	adversary	antagonist	contestant
337	289	241	107	70

enemy（n.）

❖ 片語

public enemy number one

頭號公敵

natural enemies

天敵

❖ 常用搭配詞

enemy + n.

aircraft, lines, territory, action, position, unit, troops, hands, fighter, number, forces, alien, ship, fire, army, solider, attack, propaganda, camp, defence, radar, country, bomber, front, ground, hordes, weapon, base.

adj. + enemy

worst, public, old, common, natural, main, greatest, political, dangerous, arch, external, traditional, foreign, powerful, defeated, deadly, sworn, bitter, mortal, hated, former, formidable, chief, potential, implacable, principal, approaching, biggest, bad, imaginary, unseen, personal, hidden, prime, hereditary, Fascist, obvious, severe.

opponent（n.）

❖ 片語

supporters and opponents of the movement
這場運動的支持者和反對者
to break the opponent's concentration
使對手分心

❖ 常用搭配詞

adj. + opponent

political, leading, formidable, conservative, main, chief, dangerous, semi-final, democratic, tough, principal, outspoken, bitter, Communist, right-wing, worthy, potential, vigorous, likely, vocal, determined, European, taller, staunch, vociferous, possible, old, previous, imaginary, male, implacable, prominent, illustrious, strong, former, parliamentary, vanquished, original, heavier.

rival（n.）

❖ 片語

possible rivals in the market
市場上的可能對手
rivals for the championship
爭奪冠軍的對手
He is two minutes faster than his nearest rival.
他比離他最近的對手快二分鐘。

❖ 常用搭配詞

adj. + rival

main, nearest, old, local, serious, political, great, arch, potential, chief, bitter, closest, European, biggest, democratic, international, close, foreign, major, former, domestic, smaller, possible, powerful, fierce, principal, deadly, male, hated, dangerous, greatest, long-time, German, jealous, friendly, formidable, economic, obvious, defeated, Communist.

competitor（n.）

❖ 片語

competitors in the business world
生意場上的競爭對手
competitors in the show
表演的競爭對手

❖ 常用搭配詞

adj. + competitor

major, other, main, European, foreign, potential, successful, new, nearest, international, direct, British, serious, industrial, female, top, biggest, overseas, strong, fellow, leading, closest, oldest, principal, stranded, local, powerful, would-be, global, commercial.

foe（n.）

❖ 例句

France's friends and foes
法國的朋友和敵人

❖ 常用搭配詞

adj. + foe

old, common, implacable, powerful, new, potential, dangerous, terrible, formidable, powerful, defeated, human.

challenger（n.）

❖ 片語

the challenger to the Nintendo hero.
任天堂英雄的挑戰者

a close challenger for the world championship
世界冠軍賽的勁敵

❖ 常用搭配詞

adj. + challenger

main, British, nearest, serious, only, right-wing, mandatory, conservative, leading, closest, strong, local, major, latest.

contender（n.）

❖ 片語

a serious contender for the gold medal
認真的金牌競爭者

❖ 常用搭配詞

adj. + contender

main, learning, other, serious, strong, possible, top, genuine, obvious, worthy, real, principal, major, democratic, likely, British, unsuccessful, interesting, young.

contender for +（det.）n.

title, leadership, honor, presidency, power, crown, job, post, gold, deputy, power, office, promotion.

adversary（n.）

❖ 片語

to overthrow ones' adversary
推翻某人的敵人
to confront one's adversary in a narrow pass
冤家路窄

❖ 常用搭配詞

adversary + n.

politics, system, relationship, party, style, nature, process, model.

adj. + adversary

old, ancient, new, main, formidable, powerful, human, Syrian, principal, potential,regional, worthy, long-term.

antagonist（n.）

❖ 例句

The USSR remained a dangerous antagonist.
蘇俄依然是危險的敵手。

❖ 常用搭配詞

adj. + antagonist

specific, principal, selective, competitive, dangerous, old, imaginary, potential, natural, powerful, potent, religious, fated, ferocious, future.

contestant（n.）

❖ 例句

The 25 contestants came from different colleges.
這25位參賽者來自不同的大學。

❖ 常用搭配詞

adj. + contestant

other, both, more, regional, female, postal, hopeful, local, weakest, major, skilled.

n. + contestant

other, both, more, regional, each, female, postal, hopeful, local, weakest, major, skilled, fellow, unsuccessful, vulnerable, eligible, electoral, American, superb, outside, lucky, prepared, early, losing, helmeted, youngest, potential, hard-bitten, anxious, academic.

綜合整理

enemy	有痛恨、加害、反對、競爭的意念或態度的人或國家，如敵國（the enemy）。
opponent	在比賽、遊戲、辯論、打鬥中想打敗的對象。
rival	在運動比賽、商場、或打鬥等競爭的人或團體，與competitor相似。
competitor	個人、團隊、或公司的競爭對手。另外也指參加比賽的競爭者。
foe	文學用字。意義等於enemy。
challenger	挑戰者，尤其是在如拳擊等運動中挑戰衛冕者的人。
contender	與某人或某事物競爭的人或事物，如強勁的對手（a strong contender）。
adversary	正式用字。表示和你打仗或競爭的國家或人，如宿敵（old adversary）。與opponent相似。
antagonist	比賽、戰爭、或爭吵的對手。
contestant	參加比賽的人。

Unit 13 敵意的，惡意的

StringNet語料庫出現次數

hostile	unfriendly	malevolent	belligerent
1605	176	138	109

hostile（adj.）

❖ 片語

a hostile environment
充滿敵意的環境

❖ 常用搭配詞

hostile + n.

takeover, environment, bid, forces, world, attitude, reception, response, territory, action, reaction, audience, crowd, atmosphere, feelings, bidder, criticism, behavior, critics, tribes, public, intent, place, climate, view, witness, force, eyes, look, activity, mob, society, intention, nature, tone, comment, image, relation, demonstration, headline, situation, surrounding, site, government, press.

hostile to +（det.）n.

idea, government, regime, interests, religion, Communist, Liberalism, outsiders, foreigner, life, king, league, notion, principle, existence, nationalist.

unfriendly（adj.）

❖ 片語

be environmentally unfriendly
不環保的

❖ 常用搭配詞

unfriendly + n.
act, place, voice, staff, territory, glance, eyes, stance, climate, look, comment, tone, hotel, sheepdog.

malevolent（adj.）

❖ 片語

a malevolent glare/gaze/stare
不懷好意的眼神

❖ 常用搭配詞

malevolent + n.
force, spirit, look, smile, shepherd, world, glare, glance, stare, gaze, author, intention.

belligerent（adj.）

❖ 片語

a belligerent adolescent
叛逆的青少年

❖ 常用搭配詞

belligerent + n.
attitude, country, state, stance, manner, mood, glare, reprisal.

綜合整理

hostile	對某人含有怒意並且隨時可能與其爭吵，可形容抽象或具體的人、情境、態度、行為、言語等。另外也指敵方的（如hostile territory）及反對某種思想（如hostile to Communist）。
unfriendly	不友善，可形容人或地方。
malevolent	有害人的意念，常形容眼神。
belligerent	非常不友善，隨時可能採取言語或行動上的衝突。belligerent country是正式用語，表示交戰國。

Unit 14 抵達，到達

StringNet語料庫出現次數

reach	arrive
22346	13573

reach（vt.）

❖ 常用句型

S + reach + O

❖ 例句

He is good enough to reach the semi-final, but not the final.
他足以進入準決賽，但是無法進入總決賽。

❖ 常用搭配詞

reach +（det.）n.

end, top, age, point, stage, final, door, conclusion, summit, bottom, semi-final, house, ground, earth, surface, target, road, level, place, edge, city, sea, world, peak, boundary, limit, height, position, quota, people, decision, goal.

arrive（vi.）

❖ 常用句型

S + arrive + in/ at + N

❖ 例句

She arrived in New York three days ago.
她三天前抵達紐約。

❖ 常用搭配詞

arrive at +（det.）n.

destination, house, home, decision, figure, door, solution, desk, conclusion, point, compromise, hotel, time, consensus, definition, result, theory, station.

arrive in +（det.）n.

London, England, US, Paris, America, UK.

（det.）n. + arrive

police, people, ambulance, guest, order, train, men, team, party, time, car, day, moment, troop, night, help, waiter, information, food, new, passenger, baby, coffee, plane, service, ship, guest, letter, delegation, taxi, summer, aid, goods.

綜合整理

reach	及物動詞。意義包括1.到達某個空間，2.時間的進展（某件事情的發展）。
arrive	不及物動詞，後面須接介系詞才能接受詞。意義包括1.到達某個空間： arrive at + 範圍較小的地點（如車站station），arrive in + 範圍較大的地點（如國家）；2.arrive at和reach一樣可以表示一群人取得共識（如結論conclusion）；3.某個日期來臨；4.某個東西被送達（如new arrival）。

Unit 15 地區，區域

StringNet語料庫出現次數

area	region	district	zone
56487	13975	9619	3624

area（n.）

❖ 片語

an area of outstanding natural beauty
充滿自然美景的地區

❖ 常用搭配詞

n. + area

subject, catchment, surface, New York, problem, London, city, study, service, policy, development, priority, shopping, dining, storage, target, trade, work, display, research, overflow, disaster, picnic, border, parking, control, mountain, application, danger, market, farming, working, forest, business, wilderness, home, house, lounge, mining, conversation, slum, production, water, hill, street, bay, risk, exhibition, tourist, landing, language, sitting, assembly, local, sea, garden, holiday, desert, resort, harbor, gulf, trading, walking, famine, rest, recreation, traffic, south, supply, pedestrian, search, wildlife, breeding, frontier, preparation, ground, hunting, waiting, pressure, leisure, court.

adj. + area

this, rural, other, urban, large, many, particular, local, certain, new, residential, wide, main, whole, surrounding, key, geographical, specific, conversation, sensitive, central, remote, industrial, metropolitan, built-up, major, grey, inner-city, costal, deprived, total, designated, affected, assisted, extensive, inner, broad, no-go, public, favored, depressed, peripheral, safe, western, disadvantaged, separate, limited, poor, restricted, occupational, neglected, adjacent, agricultural, working-class, vulnerable, isolated, marginal, paved, damaged, outlying, clinical, mountainous, tropical, developed, environmental, exposed, marshy, commercial, populated, sitting, scenic, low-lying, inaccessible, Mediterranean, dry, offshore, continental, smoking, waiting, confined, distant, downtown, polluted, occupied, infected, postal, historic, humid, military.

region（n.）

❖ 例句

the Asia-Pacific region

亞太地區

❖ 常用搭配詞

adj. + region

this, northern, different, autonomous, central, polar, whole, peripheral, mountainous, industrial, costal, developed, tropical, surrounding, European, Scottish, upstream, polarizing, oriental, administrative, metropolitan, arctic, agricultural, Mediterranean, urban, prosperous, unknown, equatorial, native, affected, lower, outlying, industrialized, unstable, Alpine, disputed, disadvantaged, economic, polluted, localized, adjacent, remote, British, natural, anterior, electoral, turbulent, maritime, zoogeographical, hilly, cultural, warmer, climatic, corn-growing, nuclear, star-forming, isolated, inland, dry.

n. + region

Lothian, London, coast, interaction, midland, border, east, Thames, gulf, promoter, highland, coding, mountain, brain, city, back, world, control, head, desert, Amazon, source, valley, transition, mining, manufacturing, home, forest, operating, terminal, boundary, Africa, frontier, hemisphere.

district（n.）

❖ 片語

the central business district of a city
市中心的商業區

❖ 常用搭配詞

n. + district

Edinburgh, peak, Hampshire, valley, health, US, business, lake, Lothian, forest, New York, enumeration, police, school, London, shopping, mining, slum, south, authority, polling, county, park, registration, Oxford.

adj. + district

rural, urban, metropolitan, eastern, local, federal, military, central, southern, residential, electoral, red-light, financial, designated, industrial, working-class, commercial, adjacent, postal.

district + n.

council, judge, auditor, health authority, officer, court, nurse, general hospital, attorney, chief, registry, secretary, executive, committee, leader, governor, management, boundary, chairman, visitor, police.

zone（n.）

❖ 片語

special economic zone
經濟特區
air exclusion zone
禁飛區

❖ 常用搭配詞

n. + zone

enterprise, time, war, security, subduction, air exclusion, buffer, relegation, twilight, canal, danger, battle, trade, drop, fault, protection, combat, frontier, pedestrian, transition, disaster, safety, processing, no-fly, border, fishing, emergency, fault, earthquake, supply, comfort, export, mountain, handicap, quarantine.

adj. + zone

economic, no-fly, controlled, coastal, unsaturated, free-trade, demilitarized, proliferative, nuclear-free, military, neutral, industrial, climatic, projective, forbidden, dropping, western, transitional, narrow, dead, infected, inner, restricted, Russian, American, weapon-free, vulnerable, peripheral, tropical, duty-free, no-go, smoke-free, smoking.

綜合整理

area	1.一個國家或城鎮的某一部分，2.房子或花園中有特定用途的某一部分，3.某個平面所占的面積。
region	和area相似，但指一個國家或全世界某個較大的區域，出現在region前面的形容詞和出現在area前面的形容詞有許多是一樣的，但不一定都能交替使用，例如region的範圍較大，所以前面可以出現國家名稱和自然界地形氣候相關的形容詞。另外有些慣用語如grey area也不能以region取代。
district	1.城鎮或郊區的一部分，2.國家或城市正式劃分的行政區。前面常接城市名稱（如Edinburgh district和Hamilton district），後面常接名詞表示該區内的行政機關或人員（如district council和district police）。前面出面的形容詞有許多是和area及region一樣的，但是出現次數比前面二者少很多（如urban district和metropolitan district）。
zone	和周遭環境不同的區域。常指規劃為某用途的區域（例如pedestrian zone和special economic zone）或某種特殊狀況的區域（如war zone和earthquake zone）。注意：region前面接國家名稱如British region指的是該國的區域，但是zone前面接國家名稱如American zone可能指的是在某一地區或國家由美國占領的區域，二者意義不同。
以上四個單字前面出面的形容詞和名詞有許多是一樣的，但是在語料庫的出現頻率不一樣。	

Unit 16 帝王，君王

StringNet語料庫出現次數

king	emperor	ruler	monarch	sovereign
17019	2344	1558	981	532

king（n.）

❖ 例句

The lion is the king of the jungle.
獅子是叢林之王。
Henry VIII, King of England
英國國王亨利八世

❖ 常用搭配詞

King of n.

England, France, Scotland, kings, Prussia, Denmark, Bohemia, Jerusalem, heaven, arms, rock, beasts, Holland, Troy, terrors.

King of the + n.

Jews, Mercians, Franks, universe, west, mountains, Roman, castle, road, slum, world, jungle, fairies, island, wind.

adj. + king

young, French, new, English, old, late, dead, Persian, high, former, present, great, local, exiled, Gipsy, early, deposed, future, rightful, reignine, captive, ancient, Catholic, legitimate, splendid, contemporary, ignoble.

emperor（n.）

❖ 片語

Holy Roman Emperor
神聖羅馬帝國國王
the Emperor Joseph II
約瑟夫二世國王
the Emperor Constantius II
康士坦丁二世大帝

❖ 常用搭配詞

the + adj. emperor

Roman, Byzantine, new, German, eastern, French, late, Christian, Japanese, young, current, reigning, Chinese, mogul, present, ancient, Saxon, ruling, deposed, elected, future.

ruler（n.）

❖ 例句

Who was the ruler of Egypt in 1888？
西元1888年埃及的統治者是誰？

❖ 常用搭配詞

adj. + ruler

new, secular, military, other, enlightened, Communist, Christian, strong, effective, colonial, sole, European, sovereign, supreme, power, medieval, present, legitimate, previous, local, Moslem, hereditary, British, virtual, absolute, rightful, eighteen-century, dependent, dead, foreign, unworthy, traditional, unsuccessful, unchallenged, successive, existing, nominal, real, indigenous, barbarian, autocratic, benevolent, paramount, female, elected, deposed, ancient, soldierly, genetic, imperial, cruel, historical, native, benign, authoritarian, democratic.

monarch（n.）

❖ 例句

Ingleborough— the‘ Monarch of the Dales’— is a noble hill.
英格爾伯勒，意思是「山谷的君主」，是一座壯麗的山。

❖ 常用搭配詞

adj. + monarch

absolute, constitutional, British, reigning, English, European, hereditary, fellow, exiled, divine, Catholic, beloved, radiant, future, Christian, earlier, potential, cultivated, dead, elected, individual, deposed, foreign, fallen, feudal, former, ruling, successive, ruritanian, feudal, enlightened.

monarch of +（det.）n.

Dales, range, world’s past, period, state.

sovereign（n.）

❖ 片語

the supreme authority of the sovereign
元首的至高權力

❖ 常用搭配詞

the + adj. sovereign

British, new, original, political, visiting, royal, rightful, old, native, Catholic, anointed.

sovereign of +（the）n.

United Kingdom, Spain, House of Stuart, realm, state, equal authority.

綜合整理

king	國王，皇家世襲的男性統治者。也指抽象含意如the king of rock表示最優秀或勢力最大。
emperor	帝王，統治多個國家組成的帝國。也是皇家世襲的男性統治者，後面常接姓氏（如the Emperor Dieter IV）。東方國家的君王大多稱為emperor 而不是king，king多半用在西方國家。
ruler	一個國家或地區的正式統治者，例如國王或王后。
monarch	君主立憲制的國王或王后，統治一個國家的領土，世襲且終身職。也可以用作抽象比喻，形容一座高山傲視周圍的群山（如前面❖例句Ingleborough— the' Monarch of the Dales'— is a noble hill.）。
sovereign	正式用字，指國王或王后，也可能是一個國家掌權的議會或委員會。但是在語料庫中常用來表示一個主權獨立的國家（如sovereign state, sovereign body等。）

Unit 17 帝國

StringNet語料庫出現次數

kingdom	empire	realm
6759	3784	1294

kingdom（n.）

❖ 例句

the kingdom of heaven
天國
the United Kingdom of Great Britain
大英帝國
the magic kingdom
魔術的國度

❖ 常用搭配詞

n. + kingdom

animal, congress, plant, elf, vegetable, client, vandal, mountain, twilight, mineral, fairy, reptile, bird.

adj. + kingdom

new, middle, Frankish, old, united, whole, coming, northern, Scottish, heavenly, ancient, eternal, enchanted, fictitious.

empire（n.）

❖ 片語

the Ottoman Empire
奧圖曼帝國
the Holy Roman Empire
神聖羅馬帝國

❖ 常用搭配詞

n. + empire
business, Liverpool, media, Maxwell, dwarf, publishing, world, land, trading, communication, retailing, press, electronics, bond, entertainment, shipping, newspaper.

adj. + empire
British, Roman, Ottoman, Russian, Soviet, Persian, old, whole, Chinese, western, Japanese, ancient, former, colonial, Tsarist, early, vast.

realm（n.）

❖ 片語

the copper coin of the realm
王國的銅幣
the realm of fantasy
奇幻王國

❖ 常用搭配詞

n. + of the realm

defence, peer, estate, coin, keeper, peace, community, council, good, treasurer, protector, sovereign, custom, safety, law, business, government.

綜合整理

kingdom	泛指由世襲的國王或王后統治的國家，也引申為範圍廣大的抽象疆界（如animal kingdom和the Kingdom of Heaven）。
empire	通常不只一個國家，而是數個由獨一的君王統治的國家組成的帝國。也可指由一個人建立控管的龐大組織（例如business empire和media empire）。
realm	通常表示領域或範圍，表示帝國時，只用在文學用語。

Unit 18 跌倒

StringNet語料庫出現次數

fall	trip	tumble
26223	5503	833

fall（vi.）

❖ 常用句型

S + fall（+prep. +N）

❖ 例句

The old man fell down the stairs and broke his leg.
這老人跌下樓梯，摔斷了腿。
He lost his balance and fell down.
他失去平衡，然後摔倒。

❖ 常用搭配詞

fall flat on +（det.）n.
floor, face, belly, back, hands.

trip（vi.）

❖ 常用句型

S + trip（+prep. +N）

❖ 例句

He tripped over a stone and nearly fell over.
他絆到一塊石頭，差點跌倒。

He tripped the running pickpocket with his leg and helped catch the thief.
他用腿絆倒正在逃跑的扒手，協助逮捕了那個賊。

❖ 常用搭配詞

trip over +（det.）n.

feet, shoes, boots, furniture, summat, something, tool, groceries, duck, root, leg, body, electric cable, kerb, bucket, stone, log, chair.

tumble（vi.）

❖ 常用句型

S + tumble（+prep. +N）

❖ 例句

He tumbled over and hit his knees.
他絆倒而傷膝蓋受傷。

He tumbled over the dog.
他絆到那隻狗。
The child tumbled down into the hole.
這孩子跌落到洞裏面。

❖ 常用搭配詞

人 tumble down into +（det.）n.
well, hole, tunnel, river.

人 tumble over +（det.）n.
tea-table, fence, line.

綜合整理

fall	泛指跌倒，尤其是失去平衡的結果（例如slip/ stumble/ trip and fall），後面常接down或over等副詞。
trip	表示被某物絆到而跌倒或者幾乎跌倒，也可當及物動詞，表示使絆倒。
tumble	包含整個人滾動墜落或失去控制的意思，後面可接over + 名詞，表示被某物絆倒。
在此僅討論主詞是人的情況。	

Unit 19 顛倒，反轉

StringNet語料庫出現次數

reverse	invert
2230	129

reverse（vi./vt.）

❖ 常用句型

S + reverse（+ O（+ prep. + N））

❖ 例句

Had the positions been reversed, he would have done the same for her.
如果他們的處境對調，他也會對她做同樣的事。

❖ 常用搭配詞

reverse +（det.）n.

trend, decision, process, order, effect, decline, role, situation, car, policy, action, image, damage, pattern, verdict, sign, procedure, form, position, burden, ban, cycle, flow, rule, course, judge, party, picture, meaning, truck.

invert（vt.）

❖ 常用句型

S + invert + O

❖ 例句

to invert the line into a circle
把線反轉成一個圓
Her trick is to invert cause and effect.
她的伎倆就是顛倒因果。

❖ 常用搭配詞

invert +（det.）n.

sense, logic, input, logic state, cause and effect, life, definition, reality, circuit, situation, assumption, process, relationship, tradition, natural sequence, truth, loaf, container, soil, hierarchy, topsoil, concept, theory, cake, saw, question, file, action, relation, press release.

綜合整理

reverse	指改變成為相反的決定、判決、程序、順序、或位置等，強調情勢發展方向的逆轉，另外也表示立場或物體擺設位置的對調（例如reverse the placement of the television and the table）。注意在英式英文中reverse the car等於美式英文的back up，表示把車子倒退行駛，而非迴轉。
invert	是正式用字，指改變成為相反的立場、順序、方向、關係。也指改變物體的本身的形態，例如上下顛倒或裡外相反，也指相連二物件前後順序的逆轉（例如Invert the subject and the verb to form an interrogative.）。

Unit 20 頂峰

StringNet語料庫出現次數

top	peak	summit	crest	pinnacle	acme
14938	3695	2487	675	289	49

top（n.）

❖ 例句

Write your name at the top of the answer sheet.
把你的名字寫在答案紙上方。

❖ 常用搭配詞

on top of +（det.） n.

world, pops, each other, wall, table, head, hill, cake, pile, blotter, box, filing, mountain, pipes, stove, bag, water, roof, cupboard, counter, monitor, rock, books, job, building, wave, pole, locker, icing, cliff, poll.

come top of the + n.

class, list, league, poll, entertainment, rankings, apostles.

peak（n.）

❖ 例句

The basketball player was at his peak.
這籃球選手現在正處於巔峰狀態。

peak and trough
波峰和波谷

❖ 常用搭配詞

v. + one's peak
reach, pass, approach, hit.

peak + n.
times, demand, performance, periods, hours, condition, experience, demand, labor, season, level, value, viewing, park, efficiency, winter, years, workload.

in the peak of + n.
condition, health, fitness.

summit（n.）

❖ 片語

the summit of Mount Everest
埃佛勒斯山的頂端

❖ 常用搭配詞

the summit of +（det.）n.

peak, hill, mountain, Ben, Everest.

crest（n.）

❖ 片語

on the crest of a wave

在海浪的頂端

at the crest of the ridge

在山脊上

❖ 常用搭配詞

on the crest of +（det.）n.

wave, hill, ridge, headland, house, dome, island, buttress, mountain.

pinnacle（n.）

❖ 片語

to reach the pinnacle of one's career

達到某人事業的頂峰

the pinnacle of the church

教堂的尖塔

❖ 常用搭配詞

pinnacle of +（det.）n.

achievement, career, success, rock, creation, scholarship, absurdity, knowledge, history, motor-sport, pain, profession, ambition, power, ascent.

v. + the pinnacle

reach, mark, represent, formalize.

acme（n.）

❖ 片語

at the acme of one's power
某人權力的頂峰
The acme of scientific knowledge
尖端科學知識

❖ 常用搭配詞

acme of +（det.）n.

uselessness, injustice, luxury, dinosaur, power, voyage, parental care, chatter, method, knowledge.

綜合整理

top	東西的最高點（如the top of the mountain），可能是一個平面（例如to sit on the top of the wall），也可指公司、機構、或行業的最高地位。
peak	指某人事物處在最佳狀態，也可指山脈的最頂尖端。peak times則是交通尖峰時段。
summit	指某人事物處在最佳狀態，也可指山脈的最頂尖端。和peak相似。後面常接山峰名稱表示某山的頂峰。Summit meeting 指政府領導人高峰會議。
crest	指最高點，包括山頂或波浪的浪峰（例如on the crest of a wave 表示非常成功）。
pinnacle	某件事情最成功、登峰造極的狀態，也可以指山峰（但是屬於文學用語）及建築物頂端的尖塔。
acme	某件事情最成功、登峰造極的狀態，是正式用字。

Unit 21 毒性的，惡毒的

StringNet語料庫出現次數

toxic	poisonous	noxious	venomous	virulent
1209	434	175	131	123

toxic（adj.）

❖ 片語

million tons of toxic waste
百萬噸有毒廢料
to emit toxic fumes
排放有毒氣體
highly toxic chemicals
劇毒化學物質

❖ 常用搭配詞

toxic + n.

waste, chemicals, substances, effects, fumes, gases, emissions, metals, pollutants, algae, level, side-effect, smoke, dump, product, residues, ammonia, water, agent, moiety, properties, releases, pesticide, liver, odorants, air, plant, element, fungi, vapor, oxygen, hazard, fish, legacy, lead, leak, contamination, ash, pollution, industry, drug.

poisonous（adj.）

❖ 片語

the poisonous effects of pollution
污染的毒害
the poisonous atmosphere of the office
辦公室的惡意氣氛

❖ 常用搭配詞

poisonous + n.

gas, snake, substance, chemical, plant, waste, creature, atmosphere, animal, fumes, species, spider, insect, saliva, carbon monoxide, bite, smoke, prawn, viper, leaves, spine, property, vapor, secretion, liquid, tree, doctrine, breath, skin, food.

noxious（adj.）

❖ 片語

the administration of noxious substances
有毒物質的管理
be overcome by noxious fumes
因毒氣失去知覺

❖ 常用搭配詞

noxious + n.

fumes, substances, stimulation, stimuli, thing, gas, chemicals, emission, smell, creature, form, effect, industry, potion.

venomous（adj.）

❖ 片語

the most venomous snake in the world
全世界毒性最強的毒蛇

a venomous glance
惡毒的一瞥

❖ 常用搭配詞

venomous + n.

snake, animal, bite, shot, attack, spine, darts, look, glance, species, tentacle, comment.

virulent（adj.）

❖ 片語

the most virulent form of the disease
這種病最致命的一種形式

a virulent attack of cholera
霍亂致命的攻擊

❖ 常用搭配詞

virulent + n.

form, attack, strain, poison, critic, bacteria, anti-semitism, opponent, virus, disease.

綜合整理

toxic	包含有毒性，或是被有毒物質汙染的，屬於生化用語。後面較少接表示動物的名詞。
poisonous	包含或產生有毒物質的，意義範圍廣泛，後面接的名詞種類也較多樣化。
noxious	正式用語，意義與toxic相似，後面較少接表示動植物的名詞。。
venomous	常用來表示內心的惡毒（例如venomous glance, venomous comment），也指毒蛇或昆蟲的毒液（名詞 = venom），意義與poisonous相似。後面較常接表示有毒液的動物或沾有毒汁的物品名詞（例如venomous darts）。
virulent	（毒性或疾病等）劇毒，快速致命的（例如virulent bacteria）。後面較常接細菌、病毒或疾病的名詞。也表示內心的惡毒（例如virulent critic, virulent opponent），但是屬於正式用字。

Unit 22 毒物、毒素

StringNet語料庫出現次數

poison	toxin	venom
975	435	270

poison（n.）

❖ 例句

The spider paralyses the prey by injecting it with poisons.
蜘蛛把毒注入獵物身體藉此使獵物癱瘓。

The queen coated the apple with poison.
這皇后把蘋果表面塗上毒藥。

❖ 常用搭配詞

poison + n.

gas, pen, pill, glands, arrow, ivy, oak, feast, idea, fangs, bait, dwarf, dart, pellet.

adj. + poison

deadly, virulent, deadliest, special, enough, chemical, pure, used, lethal, fatal, common, potent, corrosive, new, social, horticultural, American, natural, medical.

toxin（n.）

❖ 例句

Toxins produced by the yeast can result in diarrhea and abdominal pain.
酵母產生的毒可能會造成腹瀉和腹痛。

Natural toxins may be contained in foods.
自然的毒素有可能包含在食物中。

❖ 常用搭配詞

n. + toxin

cholera, pertussis, bt, syndrome, coli, beetle, diphtheria.

adj. + toxin

natural, dangerous, powerful, bacterial, different, lytic, insecticidal, new, harmful, active, fungal.

venom（n.）

❖ 例句

The venom of most spiders is harmless to human beings.
大部分蜘蛛的毒素對人體無害。

Snake venoms have different effects and work in several ways.
毒蛇的毒素有不同的影響，發作的方式也有好幾種。

❖ 常用搭配詞

n. + venom

snake, spider, viper, bee.

adj. + venom

such, more, real, undisguised, special, intoxicating, enough, pure, full, fast-acting, equal, large.

綜合整理

poison	意義範圍較廣，常指藉由吃下或喝下而造成死亡的毒物。
toxin	有毒物質，尤其指由細菌產生且導致疾病的毒物。
venom	毒蛇或昆蟲等射出的毒液。

Unit 23 獨裁者

StringNet語料庫出現次數

dictator	tyrant	despot
344	245	72

dictator（n.）

❖ 例句

My boss is a virtual dictator.
我的上司是個不折不扣的獨裁者。

a corrupt dictator
腐敗的獨裁者

❖ 常用搭配詞

adj. + dictator

former, military, Iraq, Romanian, virtual, great, Argentina, late, all-powerful, ruthless, mad, Soviet, corrupt, Veteran, Communist, fascist, right-wing, evil, enduring, old, hated, Chinese, powerful, defeated, efficient, aggressive, little, harsh, odious.

tyrant（n.）

❖ 例句

My mother is a domestic tyrant.
我媽媽是我們家的暴君。
a power-crazed tyrant
一個有權力狂的暴君

❖ 常用搭配詞

adj. + tyrant

local, Sicilian, domestic, Iraq, petty, cruel, haughty, archaic, brutal, Athenian, whimsical, old, classical, modern, direct, foul, bloody, alien, resentful, slave-driving, dreadful.

despot（n.）

❖ 片語

a temperamental despot
一位喜怒無常的暴君
the enlightened despot
開明專制君王

❖ 常用搭配詞

adj. + despot

enlightened, benevolent, Asiatic, dedicated, old, murderous, aspiring, powerful, Serbian, political, pretended, current, African.

❖ 綜合整理

dictator	專制獨裁的君王，尤其指以武力奪取政權的人。也指霸道、喜歡使喚別人的人。
tyrant	專制且殘暴的獨裁君王，也指殘暴不公的掌權者。
despot	與tyrant相似，但較少用。

Unit 24 賭博，打賭

StringNet語料庫出現次數

bet	gamble	wager
2091（v.），958（n.）	231（v.），436（n.）	65（v.），102（n.）

bet（vt.）

❖ 常用句型

S + bet（+ somebody）that 子句
S + bet（+ something）on something

❖ 例句

I bet you ten dollars that they won't tell you.
我跟你賭十塊錢他們不會告訴你。
He bet his entire money on the horse.
他把所有的錢都賭在這批馬上。

❖ 常用搭配詞

bet on +（det.）n.
the toss of a coin, survival, outcome, election, day, order, race.

bet（n.）

❖ 例句

We had a bet on who would win the game.
我們在賭誰會贏這場比賽。

❖ 常用搭配詞

v. +（det.）bet
hedge, place, decide, pay.

gamble（vi.）

❖ 常用句型

S + gamble（+ that 子句）
S + gamble（+ something）on something

❖ 例句

He was gambling that they had not changed the passing code.
他賭他們還沒改變密碼。
You would be gambling with people's lives if you drunk drive.
酒駕就是拿別人的生命做賭注。

❖ 常用搭配詞

gamble on +（det.）n.

currencies, horses, power, football, potential.

gamble with +（det.）n.

life, future, possibility, thing, £6,000 of savings, job, stranger, body.

gamble（n.）

❖ 例句

He is never afraid to take a gamble.

他從來不怕孤注一擲。

❖ 常用搭配詞

a + adj. gamble

big, calculated, desperate, political, major, huge, successful, brave, high-risking.

v. +（det.）gamble

take, land, constitute, have, undertake, enjoy.

wager（vt.）

❖ 常用句型

S + wager something on something

❖ 例句

I would wager that he runs faster than you.
我會賭他跑得比你快。

They wagered their fee on one guess at each other's profession.
他們賭誰能猜對對方的職業，猜輸的人付費。

❖ 常用搭配詞

wager on +（det.）n.
one's winning, outcome.

wager（n.）

❖ 片語

a small wager
打小賭

❖ 常用搭配詞

v. +（det.）wager
lay, have, manage, volunteer, make, seek, accept.

綜合整理

bet	可當動詞或名詞，表示賭博，賭金，或和人打賭某件事情的發生。
gamble	可當動詞或名詞，表示賭博，與bet相似。另外表示孤注一擲，冒…的危險。
wager	老式用字，和gamble 相似，表示賭博。另I'll wager = I'll bet 表示有把握某件事情的發生。當名詞時表示賭金（=bet）。

Unit 25 短暫的

StringNet語料庫出現次數

brief	transient	fleeting	momentary	ephemeral	transitory
4869	417	337	292	144	130

brief（adj.）

❖ 例句

He paid a brief visit to his uncle in California.
他在加州時去拜訪了他叔叔一下子。

❖ 常用搭配詞

brief + n.

period, moment, visit, encounter, look, time, pause, glimpse, silence, smile, stay, existence, interlude, life, interval, exposure, flash, second, truce, sojourn, marriage, experience, rest, laugh, instant, hesitation, acquaintance, panic, occupation, fame, honeymoon, duration, peace, stopover, kiss, interruption, sleep.

transient（adj.）

❖ 例句

Happiness is a transient thing lasting no more than a few moments.
快樂是短暫的，持續一下而已。

❖ 常用搭配詞

transient + n.

nature, response, events, changes, phenomenon, rise, transfections, increase, hotels, expression, relaxation, elevation, errors, simulation, period, species, thing, absorption, remission, signal, conditions, illness, use, population, problem, performance.

fleeting（adj.）

❖ 例句

The poor girl had a fleeting glimpse of the new doll's house in the bedroom before she was driven away.
當這貧窮的女孩被趕走之前，她瞥見臥房裡的新娃娃屋。

❖ 常用搭配詞

fleeting + n.

moment, glimpse, second, visit, smile, instant, impression, effects, expression, thought, nature, glance, encounter, hope, views, vision, images, acquaintance, temptation, emotions, life, look, pleasure, dream.

momentary（adj.）

❖ 例句

There was a momentary hesitation before he nodded.
他點頭之前有短暫的遲疑。

❖ 常用搭配詞

momentary + n.

silence, lapse, hesitation, pleasure, confusion, vision, flicker, flash, irritation, aberration, experience, panic, pain, halt, horror, frission, release, unease, glance, doubt, inattention, pause, glimpses, thought, stillness, relief.

ephemeral（adj.）

❖ 例句

Her ephemeral interest in ballet soon came to an end.
她對芭蕾舞短暫的興趣很快就結束了。

❖ 常用搭配詞

ephemeral + n.

nature, enthusiasms, things, interest, material, existence, form.

transitory（adj.）

❖ 例句

Given the transitory nature of speech, you need to make audio recording for each interview and then transcribe what the interviewee has said.
口說語言本身說完就消失，所以你必須把所有訪談做錄音，之後把受訪者說的話轉寫成文字。

❖ 常用搭配詞

transitory + n.

income, consumption, nature, period, existence, life, stage.

❖ 綜合整理

brief	持續時間很短的。在語料庫中出現次數多是因為有其他如簡短扼要、短距離的等多種意義。
transient	正式用字。表示持續時間很短的，也指短暫居住或工作的。當名詞表示過往旅客、候鳥。
fleeting	持續時間很短的，後面通常接名詞。相當於brief。
momentary	一瞬間的。相當於brief。
ephemeral	向蜉蝣一般生存時間很短，或流行時間很短的，後面常接興趣（interest）、熱心（enthusiasm）等單字。
transitory	持續瞬息或存在時間很短的。另外也表示無常的。

以上單字brief, fleeting,和momentary表示持續時間很短的，後面的名詞常關於時間、動作、身心感受等，而transient, ephemeral,和transitory除了相同表示持續時間很短的之外，還表示本身性質瞬息消失，無法長久存在，如transient population, ephemeral form, transitory life等。

Unit 26 逃跑，逃避

StringNet語料庫出現次數

avoid	escape	flee	evade	elude	shirk
11776	5208	2043	522	307	88

avoid（vt.）

❖ 常用句型

S + avoid doing something
S + avoid + O

❖ 片語

to avoid giving offence to anybody
避免冒犯別人
to avoid someone like the plague
躲避某人像躲瘟疫一樣

❖ 常用搭配詞

avoid + n.

confusion, conflict, problems, tax, trouble, disappointment, relegation, action, duplication, accidents, confrontation, responsibility, liability, detection, contamination, delay, controversy, danger, injury, people, damage, misunderstandings, situations, mistakes, war, violence, work, embarrassment, questions, ambiguity, disruption, alcohol, disputes, pregnancy, eye contact, charges, contact, arrest, loss, competition, involvement, extremes, defeat, punishment, interference, payment, things, exposure, clashes, mention, reference, publicity, waste, repetition, offence, bankruptcy, jargon, risk, errors, congestion, infection, distortion, suspicion, collisions, conscription, pain, disaster, bias, capture, stress, pollution, water, objects, criticism, use, capital, recession, death, recollapse, meat, queues, conversation, service, taxation, marriage, bloodshed, jail, coalescence, temptation, difficulties, obstacles, failure, gossip, prosecution, issues, double-counting, revolution, extinction, leaks, spillage, rape.

avoid + the + n.

need, risk, use, problem, conclusion, possibility, issue, danger, necessity, pitfall, temptation, impression, question, consequence, greenbelt, area, word, kind, drop, trap, situation, effect, expense, cost, embarrassment, contract, commission, fate, company, term, cost, mistake, creation, sun, water, feeling, fact, excess, disaster, subject, attention, difficulties, accident, drama, rush, type, town, charge, damage, police, disadvantage, confusion, appearance, heat, extreme, car, tendency, suspicion, idea, chaos, attentions, likelihood, eyes, argument.

escape（vi./vt.）

❖ 常用句型

S + escape（+ prep. + N）
S + excape + O

❖ 例句

to escape justice

逃避司法的審判

to escape unhurt

（在災難或意外中）毫髮無傷

❖ 常用搭配詞

escape one's + n.

notice, attention, lips, clutches, eye, obligation, past, hold, predator, duty, image, marker, share, problem, liability, torment, force, constriction, influence, commitment.

escape + n.

injury, death, liability, detection, justice, police, notice, criticism, punishment, prosecution, conviction, attention, capture, destruction, arrest, prison, damage, persecution, tax, relegation, Lucy, predator, violence, poverty, assassination, danger, reality, responsibility, deportation, condemnation, discovery, blame, misrepresentation, revolution, involvement, extinction, bankruptcy, scrutiny, boredom, captivity, jail, detention.

escape from +（det.）n.

prison, hospital, car, tower, control, dilemma.

flee（vt./vi.）

❖ 常用句型

S + flee（+ prep. + N）

❖ 片語

to flee in terror
嚇跑
to flee empty hand
空手而逃

❖ 常用搭配詞

flee the + n.
country, city, scene, area, fighting, capital, family, Nazis, battlefield, house, nest, island, room, war, place.

evade（vt.）

❖ 常用句型

S + evade + O

❖ 片語

to manage to evade the press
設法避開媒體
to evade the thought of death
避免死亡的念頭
to evade the fact that
逃避某個事實

❖ 常用搭配詞

evade the + n.
issue, question, provisions, challenge, tax, clutches, home, poll, prohibition, hand, truth, act, problem, duty, danger, subject, thought, totalitarianism, scandal.

evade + n.
capture, detection, questions, arrest, tax, responsibility, liability, predators, duty, export, justice, accusations, control.

elude（vt.）

❖ 常用句型

S + elude + O

❖ 例句

She has eluded Jessica for weeks.
她躲避Jessica好幾週了。

The burglar tried to elude the police.
這夜賊躲避警察。

❖ 常用搭配詞

elude + n.
detection, capture, control, inquiry.

elude one's + n.
grasp, pursuers, contemporaries, observation, understanding, teams, attempts, predecessors, hand.

shirk（vi./vt.）

❖ 常用句型

S + shirk （+ O）

❖ 片語

to shirk one's duty/responsibility
逃避責任

❖ 常用搭配詞

shirk one's + n.
responsibilities, duty, task, work, role, obligation.

綜合整理

avoid	及物動詞。避免壞事的發生（如avoid the risk of danger），避免做某件事情（avoid getting hurt），避免接觸某人（avoid his ex-wife），或逃過某件不好的事情（如avoid an accident）。
escape	及物或不及物動詞。指逃跑以免被捉（如escape from prison），逃離危險等困境，或逃過某件不好的事情（= avoid）
flee	及物或不及物動詞。倉促逃離危險等困境。
evade	及物動詞。避開不談某件事情，逃避盡到某個責任，逃避付錢（如evade tax），或逃跑以免被捉（如evade the police）。
elude	用計逃避某人或某事（=avoid），受詞可以是人。也指錯過某事（例如Success has eluded him.）或忘記。
shirk	因懶惰而逃避責任。

Unit 27 投機的

StringNet語料庫出現次數

speculative	opportunistic
663	104

speculative（adj.）

❖ 例句

a speculative stock market
投機的股票市場
to make a speculative fortune with antiques
賣古董賺取投機財

❖ 常用搭配詞

speculative + n.
demand, building, builder, development, investment, money, bubble, fund, developer, selling, buying, exploration, stocks, venture, trading, profit, behavior, game, housing, attempt.

opportunistic（adj.）

❖ 片語

on an opportunistic basis
採機會主義態度

❖ 常用搭配詞

opportunistic + n.

infections, predator, feeder, approach, screening, grab, attitude, manner, alliance, dealer, thug, baiss, bird, seller, conformism, theft, behavior, virus.

❖ 綜合整理

speculative	商業英語用字，表示為得利益買賣而做的買賣或行動，尤指投機商業行為。
opportunistic	含負面，貶低之意。表示抓住任何機會以獲取不正當利益、權力、或錢財等。如opportunistic theft指見有機可趁而進行的偷竊行為。

Unit 28 貪心

StringNet語料庫出現次數

greedy	voracious	rapacious	avaricious	covetous
460	78	49	32	22

greedy（adj.）

❖ 片語

be dreadfully/ incurably greedy
極端/無可救藥地貪婪

❖ 常用搭配詞

greedy + n.

eyes, man, bastard, gilt, horse, tycoon, pig, party, desire, fish, creature, league, cow, child, elite, delight, discontent, looks, bird, expectation, predator, society, pursuit, smile.

greedy for +（det.）n.

excess, award, patronage, life, land, meat, possessions, food, status, business, biscuit, profit.

voracious（adj.）

❖ 例句

Johnny always has a voracious appetite for women and drink.
Johnny總是貪愛酒色。

❖ 常用搭配詞

voracious + n.
appetite, consumers, reader, blood-sucker.

rapacious（adj.）

❖ 片語

a rapacious appetite for something
對某事物貪得無厭
a rapacious landlord
貪心的房東
rapacious forms of capitalist entrepreneurship
資本主義企業家的貪婪面

❖ 常用搭配詞

rapacious + n.
landlord, demand, egoism, gods, capitalist, action, appetite, rape, strategy, relative, monster, invasion, enemy, capitalism, habit, egoist, greed, company.

avaricious（adj.）

❖ 片語

the avaricious merchant
貪財的商人
the rich and the avaricious
有錢人和貪心之輩

❖ 常用搭配詞

avaricious + n.
figure, citizen, fellow, speculator, money-lender, monarch, mediocrities.

covetous（adj.）

❖ 片語

a covetous look in one's eye
某人貪婪的眼神
finger the silk with covetous hands
手指頭貪戀地撫摸絲綢

❖ 常用搭配詞

covetous + n.
eyes, desire, rival, rule, look, finer, person, part, hand, man.

綜合整理

greedy	對食物、錢財、權力、物質等無止盡的貪心，後面常接for + 名詞。也可以指渴求，是正面意義，如 be greedy to learn指求知若渴。
voracious	主要是指對食物的貪慾，也指具有強烈的慾望去做某件事情或擁有某個東西。
rapacious	正式用字。意思和greedy相似。特別指貪求自己不需要或沒有權利得到的東西，後面常接名詞，可以是人或抽象名詞。
avaricious	正式用字。特別指貪戀財富。
covetous	正式用字。特別指貪戀別人擁有的東西。

Unit 29 彈性的

StringNet語料庫出現次數

flexible	elastic	pliable	pliant
2358	431	61	45

flexible（adj.）

❖ 片語

a flexible personality
有彈性的個性

❖ 常用搭配詞

flexible + n.

approach, working, working hours, response, response strategy, system, way, manufacturing, manufacturing system, exchange rate, use, labor force, arrangement, signoidoscopy, hours, friend, packaging, learning, wages, training opportunity, workforce, specialization, retirement, plan, hose, production, model, nature, firm, patterns, workers, instrument, range, concept, teaching, course, services, sale, means, facility, timetable, attitude, mind, manner, rostering, support, chain, facilities, work, rate, access, option, solution, budgeting, shaft, planning, procedure, exployment, diplomacy, territory, work practices, office space, neck, jobs, shool, backbone, blade, shape, player, people, thinker.

elastic（adj.）

片語

an elastic band

橡皮筋

❖ 常用搭配詞

elastic + n.

band, constants, modulus, property, deformation, response, material, tissue, recovery, tape, loop, energy, rope, cord, stockings, skin, fluid, bandage, body, drawcord, behavior, supply, strap, fiber, collision, problem, solid, labor tension, knitting, curve, model, characteristics, corset.

pliable（adj.）

❖ 片語

more pliable

比較容易曲折的

infinitely/ perfectly pliable

極度容易彎曲的

❖ 常用搭配詞

pliable + n.

rope, conscience, stem, material, government, man, American.

pliant（adj.）

❖ 片語

a pliant successor
柔順的繼位者
pliant fingernails
易彎曲的指甲

❖ 常用搭配詞

pliant + n.
features, instrument, curves, lips, judge, willow stem, editor, landlady.

綜合整理

flexible	指一個人或一個計劃能夠因時因地制宜，做適當的改變以適應情勢。也指物品有彈性。
elastic	通常指物品以橡皮等彈性材料製成的，有彈性可以伸縮的（如elastic band）。有時也表示能夠依環境而調整的。
pliable	指物品有彈性可以伸縮的。也指人容易被影響或被操弄的。
pliant	指物體柔順易變形（如pliant lips）。也指人人容易被影響或被弄的（如pliant judge沒主見的法官）。

Unit 30 坦白的，直接的

StringNet語料庫出現次數

frank	straightforward	blunt	candid
3371	1953	468	144

frank（adj.）

❖ 例句

I'll be frank with you.
我會對你坦白。
She is frank about her personal preference.
她很坦白表示她的個人偏好。
They had frank exchange of views.
他們坦誠交換意見。

❖ 常用搭配詞

frank + n.
discussion, exchange, bishop, admission, interview, appeal, account, disclosusre, admiration, astonishment, smile, revelation, disbelief, recognition, comment, assessment, manner, detail, letter, face, talk, reply, tone.

straightforward（adj.）

❖ 例句

He is straightforward with his boss.
他對上司說話很直接。
She is straightforward about her perception.
她會直接說出她的感受

❖ 常用搭配詞

straightforward + n.
question, manner, statement, explanation, fashion, answer, attempt, application, observation, command.

blunt（adj.）

❖ 片語

be fairly/ remarkably blunt
相當直率（耿直）

❖ 常用搭配詞

blunt + n.
statement, speaking, words, answer, refusal, terms, message, speech, question.

candid（adj.）

❖ 片語

remarkably/ unusually candid
相當/超乎尋常地坦率
candid expression of one's outrage
坦白表達憤怒

❖ 常用搭配詞

candid + n.
confession, discussion, gaze, expression, statement, mind, response, acknowledge, word, look.

綜合整理

frank	誠實，坦率，不隱瞞，即使是不好的事情。後面常接with + 人， about + 事情。
straightforward	雖然在語料庫出現的頻率比blunt高，但大多是表示一件事情事情單純易懂的。較少用來表示誠實不隱瞞，直言不諱，但較沒有像blunt的負面意義。。
blunt	誠實直言不諱，即使可能會得罪人，有負面意義。另外表示物體不鋒利（例如blunt instrument鈍器），人的頭腦遲鈍，衍伸為耿直、直率之意。
candid	誠實，坦率，不隱瞞，即使是不好的事情。和frank相似，後面常接with +人， about + 事情。另外也是攝影術語，也有其他意義。

Unit 31 疼痛

StringNet語料庫出現次數

pain	hurt	agony	sore	ache	pang	twinge
7981	4316（v.），217（n.）	985	782（adj.），191（n.）	387	172	112

pain（n.）

❖ 片語

aches and pains

疼痛

be at pains to do something

非常用心盡力做某事

❖ 常用搭配詞

pain in the + n.

neck, back, ass, head, chest, bum, joints, stomach, day, eyes, limbs.

v. + the pain

ease, feel, relieve, see, have, kill, make, stand, know, bear, dull, stop, ignore, overcome, endure, take, cause, fear, forget, alleviate, notice, treat.

hurt（vi.）

❖ 常用句型

S + hurt

❖ 例句

My head hurt a lot.
我的頭很痛。

❖ 常用搭配詞

adv. + hurt

badly, seriously, slightly, deeply, really easily, grievously, terribly, physically, bitterly, extremely.

（det.） n. + hurt（vi.）

love, head, throat, back, truth, area, chest, leg, past, knee, toe, hand, neck, face, tummy.

hurt（n.）

❖ 片語

to make the hurt go away
消除疼痛
the hurt in her eyes
她眼睛的疼痛

❖ 常用搭配詞

adj. + hurt

little, past, physical, great, old, bitter, real, unresolved, flaming, desperate, potent.

agony（n.）

❖ 片語

in agony

劇痛

the agony of death

死亡的劇痛

❖ 常用搭配詞

the agony of + n.

death, pseudo-injury, surgery, attrition, fire, seasickness, arthritis, numbness.

adj. + agony

such, absolute, eternal, uncontrollable, horrifying, constant, excruciating, permanent, extreme.

sore（adj.）

❖ 例句

I've got a sore back from the lifting.

我搬東西之後背很酸痛。

❖ 常用搭配詞

sore + n.

throat, thumb, head, point, tummy, subject, spot, bottom, foot, hand, tongue, trial, back, hamstring, face, temptation.

sore（n.）

❖ 片語

pressure sores on the joints
關節壓迫性疼痛

sores of inflammation
發炎痛

❖ 常用搭配詞

a sore（sores）on the + n.

lips, conscience, elbow, backs, vulva.

adj. + sore

cold, running, open, primary, little, septic, red.

ache（vi.）

❖ 例句

My grandmother said her whole body ached.
我祖母說她全身都痛。

❖ 常用搭配詞

（det.） n. + ache

head, body, legs, heart, arms, feet, muscles, back, eyes, shoulder, throat, knees, jaw, limbs, stomach, neck, face, joints, bones, teeth, breath, chest, mouth, hand, wrist, ears.

ache（n.）

❖ 片語

an ache in ones' spine/ head/ throat
脊椎/頭/喉嚨痛

❖ 常用搭配詞

ache of +（det.） n.

loss, desire, love, hunger, loneliness, uncertainty, disappointment, separation.

adj. + ache

dull, deep, throbbing, warm, funny, slight, unrelenting, relentless, hard, terrible, muscular, general, grinding.

pang（n.）

❖ 片語

birth pang
生產之痛

❖ 常用搭配詞

n. + pang

hunger, birth, anxiety, stomach.

twinge（n.）

❖ 片語

to feel a twinge of pain
感到一陣疼痛

❖ 常用搭配詞

a twinge of + n.

guilt, sadness, jealousy, envy, conscience, disappointment, regret, sympathy, pain, unease, discomfort, panic, uneasiness, anguish, nervousness.

綜合整理

此項目只探討肉體上的痛苦	
pain	可數或不可數名詞。強調疼痛的感覺。此字有許多相關成語，如a pain in the neck 指難對付或惹人厭的人或事。Be at pains to do something表示熱切或迫切地做某件事情。
hurt	可數或不可數名詞。當不及物動詞時表示主詞感覺疼痛（如My left leg hurts a lot.）。
agony	可數或不可數名詞。指劇痛，也指臨死之前的痛苦。
sore	可數名詞。因外傷或感染引起的疼痛，通常伴隨紅腫。
ache	可數名詞。強調身體部位的疼痛（如headache, stomachache等），多指持續但不甚劇烈的疼痛。
pang	指肉體上的劇痛。
twinge	可數名詞。突然的微痛，刺痛。也指一陣不舒服的情緒。
另外tender （adj.）表示一觸即痛的（如The bruise on my arm is still tender to touch.）。smart （adj.）表示引起劇痛的（如a smart slap on the face）。 另一個字distress用來表示身體劇痛的時候屬於正式用字，語料庫中只有respiratory distress和physical distress。	

Unit 32 提升

StringNet語料庫出現次數

encourage	promote	advance	boost	further
11172	6529	2865	1715	384

encourage（vt.）

❖ 常用句型

S + encourage + O

❖ 片語

to encourage the use of alternative energy
鼓勵使用替代能源
to encourage the development of non-governmental newspaper
鼓勵成立非政府報紙

❖ 常用搭配詞

encourage + n.

investment, authorities, growth, development, participation, skills, action, use, work, involvement, cooperation, behavior, research, debate, business, communication, standard, responsibility, expression, learning, protest, payment, trade, production.

promote（vt.）

❖ 常用句型

S + promote + O

❖ 片語

to promote the welfare of old people
提升老人福利
to promote economic growth
提升經濟成長

❖ 常用搭配詞

promote the + n. of

development, use, interest, idea, welfare, growth, cause, study, formation, education, provision, exchange, sale, concept, importance, work, good, employment, image, expansion, benefit, career, quality, conservation, value, improvement, survival, health, supply, involvement, establishment, integrity, coordination, adoption, teaching.

promote + n.

competition, health, growth, research, homosexuality, cooperation, peace, equality, trade, awareness, sales, democracy, efficiency, discussion, change, education, tourism, business, investment, independence, development, employment, opportunity, quality, contact, activity, understanding, stability, symmetry, improvement, fertility, reform, learning, respect, harmony, innovation, freedom.

advance（vi./vt.）

❖ 常用句型

S + advance（+ O）

❖ 例句

to advance the cause of democracy
促進民主目標
to advance the interests of all labors
促進勞工利益

❖ 常用搭配詞

advance +（det.） n.
cause, career, interests, creation, idea, education, aim, understanding, process, well-being, technique, number, integration, polarization, development, hegemony, status, relationship.

n. + has/ have advanced
technology, society, life.

boost（vt.）

❖ 常用句型

S + boost + O

❖ 片語

to boost one's income
增加收入
to boost the use of renewable resources
推動使用再生能源

❖ 常用搭配詞

boost + one's n.

confidence, morale, chance, income, ego, performance, image, share, success, hope, economy, popularity, profit, career, presence, vote, funds, self-esteem.

boost the + n.

number, value, power, morale, chance, production, supply, image, speed, role, performace, use, provision, circulation, rank, output, prospect.

further（vt.）

❖ 常用句型

S + further + O

❖ 片語

to further the mission of the foundation
推動基金會的使命
to further the interests of the members
增進會員的利益

❖ 常用搭配詞

further the + n.

cause, interest, aim, process, sale, development, mission, use, knowledge, peace, spread, career, belief.

綜合整理

encourage	提升某件事情（可能是正面或負面的事情）存在、發生、或發展的可能性，受詞是某件事情。另有鼓舞、鼓勵之意，受詞可能是人或組織機構。
promote	幫助某件事情發展或增加，也指提倡某種想法使人支持某件事情。受詞是某件事情，不能是人。
advance	及物或不及物動詞。表示發展，改善，如知識的提升或科技的進步。受詞是某件事情，不能是人。
boost	使某件事情增加或進步以致於成功，也指提升某人的某種心態（如信心confidence）。
further	幫助某件事情進步或成功，與promote相似。受詞是某件事情，不能是人。

Unit 33 提高

StringNet語料庫出現次數

raise	lift	heighten	elevate
19076	6683	472	428

raise（vt.）

❖ 常用句型

S + raise + O

❖ 例句

He raised his hand to ask for help.
他舉手求助。

❖ 常用搭配詞

raise one's + n.

head, eyebrow, hand, eyes, glass, voice, arm, hat, wing, fist, sword, face, cup, gaze, bowl, finger.

raise the + n.

level, possibility, profile, price, standard, defence, cost, temperature, quality, status, rate, awareness, number, consciousness, value, wage, hope, expectation, risk, spirit, tone, height, morale, pitch, share, proportion, supply, image, visibility, chance, score, power, efficiency, likeliness, amount, threat, stake, probability, effectiveness.

lift（vt.）

❖ 常用句型

S + lift + O

❖ 例句

She lifted her head and looked at them.
她抬起頭來看著他們。
He lifted the lid of the jar.
他打開罐子的蓋子。

❖ 常用搭配詞

lift +（det.） n.

lid, head, hand, receiver, finger, state, phone, veil, spirit, latch, blocade, title, world, trophy, cup, body, dog, arm, face, eyes, weights, child, share, glass, sheet, cover, curtain, hair, kettle, bike, level, roof, baby, car, tray, girl, immunity, bag, bottom, boat, tail, scale, award, sanction, sales, spirit, trade, power, ceiling, bottle, price, knife, patien, chair, gun, economy.

heighten（vt.）

❖ 常用句型

S + heighten + O

❖ 片語

fears heightened by the hostage's death
因為人質死亡而加深的恐懼
to heighten the feelings of tension and despair
提高緊張和失望的感受

❖ 常用搭配詞

heighten +（det.）n.

sense, tension, awareness, effect, suspicion, profile, importance, anticipation, poignancy, feeling, atmosphere, consciousness, urge, perception, expectation, suspicion, involvement, difference, attraction, contradiction, sensitivity.

elevate（vt.）

❖ 常用句型

S + elevate + O

❖ 例句

to elevate the status of contemporary drama
提高當代戲劇的地位
to elevate bad taste into an art form
把不良的品味提升到藝術的形式

❖ 常用搭配詞

elevate +（det.）n.

status, host, concept, tone, student, politics, authority, subject, system, inscription, literature, patient, finance, humor, probability, body, limbs, people, morbidity, route, level.

綜合整理

raise	把某物提升到較高的空間位置，強調位置的改變。也表示提高數量、程度。受詞可以是具體或抽象名詞（如raise one's voice提高音量）。
lift	把某人或某物往上提舉，強調提舉的動作，如將人抱起、掀舉容器的蓋子等。也指抬高身體某個部位，此義與raise相同。另外也指提高價錢或利潤等。
heighten	提高、強化某種情緒或效果，受詞通常是抽象名詞，且時常是負面的意義。
elevate	屬於正式用字。1.提高某人事物的地位，2.把某物提升到較高的空間位置，3.在科技術語上表示提高數量、溫度，壓力等。

Unit 34 挑剔的，拘泥小節的

StringNet語料庫出現次數

meticulous	fussy	fastidious	finicky	picky
284	190	108	34	23

meticulous（adj.）

❖ 例句

She cleaned the room with meticulous care.
她非常仔細地打掃房間。
He is meticulous in his choice of words.
他非常講究用字遣詞。

❖ 常用搭配詞

meticulous + n.

care, detail, attention, planning, work, research, record, account, preparation, scrutiny, organization, craftsmanship, observance, approach, survey, accuracy, painting, player, selection, hierarchy, reconstruciton.

fussy（adj.）

❖ 例句

She is fussy about her weight.
她對自己的體重很挑剔。
a fussy neighbor
挑剔的鄰居

❖ 常用搭配詞

fussy + n.

way, investor, mess, toss, eater, brother, detail, neighbor, manner, gardener, movement, referee, bow, teacher, clothes.

fastidious（adj.）

❖ 片語

be fastidious about personal hygiene
過分在乎個人衛生
excessively fastidious
極度講究

❖ 常用搭配詞

fastidious + n.

member, organism, impression, producer, taste, sequence, customer, detail, imagination, attitude, manner, sense, concern, corporal, fiancés.

finicky（adj.）

❖ 例句

He was being too finicky.
他太小題大作。
finicky detailed work
精緻巧妙的作品

❖ 常用搭配詞

finicky + n.

stuff, business, gentleman, manner, feeder, observation.

picky（adj.）

❖ 例句

She is such a picky person that everything has to be perfect.
她相當吹毛求疵，每件事情都要求完美。

be picky about social status
講究社會地位

❖ 常用搭配詞

picky + n.

eater, finger, person.

綜合整理

meticulous	非常注重細節的，可形容人或非人。
fussy	過度注重細微、不重要的細節，很難被取悅。也指物品製作很繁複，通常有貶損之意。另外也指動作精細的。可形容人或非人。
fastidious	非常注重細節，很難被取悅。可形容人或非人。
finicky	過度注重細微、不重要的細節。也指動作精細的。可形容人或非人。
picky	只偏愛某些東西，很難被取悅。通常只用來形容人。

Unit 35 挑選

StringNet語料庫出現次數

choose	select
16391	5722

choose（vi./vt.）

❖ 常用句型

S + choose（+ somebody/ something）to do something
S + choose（+ somebody/ something）as something
S + choose + prep. + N

❖ 片語

to choose the moment to do sth
選擇某時刻做某事

to choose somebody as one's partner
選擇某人為合夥人

to choose between A and B
在 A和B之間做選擇

to choose at random
隨機挑選

❖ 常用搭配詞

choose to + v.

do, use, ignore, live, go, make, take, have, work, stay, represent, give, play, call, leave, spend, study, remain, move, become, write, follow, believe, enter, visit, wear, act, adopt, joing, support, accept, travel, speak, investigate, help, attend.

choose the right + n.

time, people, words, moment, kind, car, person, place, bait, sort, shampoo, road, ones, point, agent.

choose +（det.）n.

name, career, time, place, day, site, government, subject, type, form, date, course, option, chair, route, theme, leader, way, path, topic, color, area, wife, man, moment, house, mate, school, candidate, life, example, president, winner, title, means, person, position.

select（vt.）

❖ 常用句型

S + select somebody（for something）
S + select somebody to do something
S + select somebody/ something as something
S + select somebody/ something from something

❖ 例句

This is the third time he has been selected as their class leader.
這是他第三次被選為班代。

The subjects for the experiment were selected at random.
這個實驗的受試者是隨機挑選的。

❖ 常用搭配詞

select the correct + n.

word, answer, information, medium, temperature, form, city, diet, tool, size.

select the right + n.

person, coverage, type, personnel, tone, question, people, measure, treatment, machine, part, consultant.

n. + selected for

schools, selection, patients, women, companies, players, variables, cell.

select + n.

candidates, patients, items, areas, books, schools, committees, individuals, subjects, students, modules, children, technology, plant, employees, methods, materials, delegates, groups, goods, topics, foods, samples, words, companies, teams, examples, targets, respondents, options, names, films, cases, architects.

綜合整理

choose	及物或不及物動詞。Choose to + Vroot表示由個人意志決定去做某件事情。意義和select相似，但強調選擇個人偏好，如be able to pick and choose one's customers表示可以隨自己偏好選擇顧客而不必全部接受。
select	及物動詞。常用在被動語態。意義和select相似，但強調選擇認為是最好的（如to select on the basis of seniority）。

Unit 36 跳躍

StringNet語料庫出現次數

jump	leap	spring	hop	vault
4922	2001	1698	522	147

jump（vi./vt.）

❖ 常用句型

S + jump（+ adv.）（+ perp. + N）
S + jump + O

❖ 片語

to jump ship
跳槽
to jump to conclusion
過早下定論
bungee jump
高空彈跳

❖ 常用搭配詞

jump + adv.

up, out, down, in, back, off, on, around, over, ahead, away, right, forwards, backwards, ashore, quickly, violently, sideways, suddenly, aboard, directly, nimbly, superbly.

jump + prep.

to, on, from, into, at, in, off, over, for, by, onto, through, as, with, like, between,across, under, around, about, without, behind, inside, astride, above, upon, against.

jump the + n.

gun, queue, ditch, gap, housing, rails, waves, wagon.

leap（vi./vt.）

❖ 常用句型

S + leap + adv. / perp. + N

❖ 例句

Flames leapt up the chimney.
火焰從煙囪竄出來。
She could feel her heart leap into her throat.
她感覺她的心臟跳到她的喉嚨。

❖ 常用搭配詞

（det）n. + leap

heart, flames, car, profit, man, mind, cat, quantum, dog, pulse, salmon, people, shadow, eyes, share, body, fish, desire, time, figure, light, frog, stomach, Kathrine（human names）, panic, membership.

leap + adv.

forward, away, ahead, straight, ashore, right, instantly, overboard, again, across, lightly, aside, excitedly, nimbly, vividly, high, tall, clear, upwards, easily, backwards, sideways, enormously, gigantically, treacherously, directly, spontaneously.

leap + prep.

to, from, into, at, in, on, off, over, with, onto, across, through, like, toward, upon, up, between, down, inside, around, within, after, under, about.

spring（vi.）

❖ 常用句型

S + spring + adv. / perp. + N

❖ 片語

examples that spring to mind
突然想到的例子
to spring up from one's seat
從座位上跳起來

❖ 常用搭配詞

spring + adv.

up, out, back, forward, away, apart, immediately, fully, down, aside, off, spontaneously, upright, upward, suddenly, nimbly, readily, forth.

spring + prep.

from, to, into, on, at, in, for, with, by, of, through, upon, off, onto, toward, against.

（det.）n. + spring

tears, hair, ideas, breeze, hand, water, light, question, people, leaf, name, concept, words, horse, tree, hope, tiger.

hop（vi.）

❖ 常用句型

S + hop（+ adv.）（+ prep. + N）

❖ 片語

to hop from one foot to the other
邊跳邊走
to hop on one leg
單腳跳

❖ 常用搭配詞

hop + adv.

away, nimbly, inside, lightly, gently, close, rapidly, slowly, tentatively.

hop + prep.

on, from into, to, over, in, across, off, onto, between, toward, around, about, like, through.

（det.） n. + hop

birds, Mildred（human names）, doctor, flesh, frog, cargo, dancer.

Vault（vi.）

❖ 常用句型

S + vault + prep. + N

❖ 例句

He vaulted cleanly through the open window.

他俐落地手臂一撐就跳過敞開的窗戶。

to vault over the counter

手臂一撐跳過櫃台

❖ 常用搭配詞

vault + prep.

over, with, in, into, on, at, like, within, from.

vault + adv.

over, up, down, throughout, on, straight, one-handed, cleanly, aboard, promptly.

（det.） n. + vault

he, she, fragments.

綜合整理

jump	往上跳，跳過某物或跳離開某物，也指從高處跳下。和leap一樣指突然快速朝某方向移動（如jump back, jump in the car等）。常用作不及物動詞，後面接over, across, onto, out of等介系詞，但指跳過某物時也可以是及物動詞（如jump the fence），另有片語如jump the gun指迫不及待，jump the queue表示插隊。主詞通常是人或動物。
leap	和jump一樣表示往上跳，特別強調奮力一跳，但是通常著地在不同的位置。不及物動詞，後面一定接介系詞或副詞。但指跳過某物時也可以是及物動詞（如leap the fence）。主詞可以是有形物質（如heart, car）、自然界的光影、火、人、動物、或profit（利潤）、time（時間）等抽象名詞。
spring	突然朝前方或往上彈跳，也指受壓後彈回，或突然出現（如spring out at somebody）。不及物動詞，後面一定接介系詞或副詞。主詞通常是有形物質（如tears）、動物、或想法等抽象名詞，較少是人。
hop	單腳跳，或昆蟲或鳥類等快速而小步跳走。在口語中表示快速或突然移動（如hop in）。不及物動詞。主詞通常是人或動物。
vault	用手臂或竿子支撐跳過某物。另外和leap可指排名或水準的往上提高。不及物動詞。土詞通常是人。

Unit 37 停止

StringNet語料庫出現次數

stop	cease	suspend	halt
23651	2923	2326	1441

stop（vi./vt.）

❖ 常用句型

S + stop（+ O）
S + stop to do something
S + stop doing something

❖ 例句

Please stop doing that.
請停止那樣做。
When they reached a gas station they stopped to ask the directions.
他們經過加油站時停下來問路。

❖ 常用搭配詞

stop + Ving

talking, working, playing, doing, using, breathing, laughing, taking, trying, thinking, making, going, looking, speaking, smoking, loving, seeing, paying, coming, moving, running, shaking, giving, having, selling, raining, arguing, asking, eating, fighting, reading, singing, writing, buying, calling, feeling, saying, crying, drinking, believing, shouting, telling, pretending, behaving, growing, producing, wearing, treating.

（det.） n. + stop

people, time, bus, heart, way, rain, train, attempt, car, police, man, hand, music, power, order, driver, government, effort, voice, engine, action, campaign, injunction, bus, water, world, process, desire, emergency, work.

cease（vi./vt.）

❖ 常用句型

S + cease（+ O ）
S + cease to do something
S + cease doing something

❖ 例句

Her response never ceases to amaze me.
她的反應總是讓我感到驚奇。
The factory has ceased to exist.
這工廠已經不存在了。
All conversation ceased and everyone in the restaurant turned around.
所有的交談都停下來，餐廳裡的每一個人都轉過頭來。

❖ 常用搭配詞

cease + to Vroot/ Ving

to exist, to have, trading, to function, to amaze, to work, to apply, to believe, to operate, to use, to hold, to act, to play, using, to trade, to matter, to think, to do, to care, to become, to carry, to serve, to enjoy, to make, to run, feeding, operating, to occupy, to pay.

cease + n.

production, operations, fire, publication, hostilities, work, attack, contact, growth, employment, payment, business, treatment, recognition, childbearing, payment.

（det.） n. + cease

conversation, wind, operation, group, mine, cries, mumblings.

suspend（vt.）

❖ 常用句型

S + suspend + O

❖ 例句

The basketball player was suspended for two matches for his assault.
這籃球球員因為攻擊他人而被停賽二次。
The volunteers of the IRA will temporarily suspend hostile military operations on Chirtmas Eve for eight hours.
愛爾蘭志願軍在聖誕夜停止敵對軍事行動八小時。

❖ 常用搭配詞

（det.）+ n. be suspended

constitution, shares, registration, certificate, sentence, policy, officers, office, activity, work, sailing, trading, time, operation, trade, talk, cross, association, program, investigation, staff, conference, act, action, Stewart（human name）, services, life, case, council, process, court, trial, order, director.

suspend from + n.

practice, duty, office, school, work, membership, government, club.

halt（vi. /vt.）

❖ 常用句型

S + halt + O

❖ 片語

in an effort to halt the spread of HIV among heterosexuals

竭力遏止愛滋病在同性戀者之間傳染

in an attempt to halt recession

企圖挽回經濟衰退

❖ 常用搭配詞

halt the + n.

fighting, spread, slide, expansion, process, flow, decline, trial, work, growth, development, advance, violence, destruction, sale, use, attack, fall, onset, march, deployment, progress, killing, supply, haemorrhage, start, production, bloodshed, disease, conflict, construction, deterioration.

（det.） n. + have halted

government, judge, company, fighting, Japan, troops, masses, demonstrators, strike.

綜合整理

stop	及物或不及物動詞。表示1.（使）靜止不動，2.不再繼續做某件事情（stop + Ving），或3.停止原有的動作（活動）以開始做某件事情（stop to + Vroot），也就是說後面可接不定詞（to + Vroot）或動名詞（Ving），但是意義不相同。
cease	及物或不及物動詞。正式用字，也是法律用字。表示停止做某件事情，或某件事情停止發生，後面可接不定詞（to + Vroot）或動名詞（Ving），意義相同，但在語料庫中接不定詞（to + Vroot）的用法佔大多數。
suspend	及物動詞。正式暫時停止某件持續已久的事情。也表示因為行為不檢而被暫時停職或休學。常用被動語態。
halt	及物或不及物動詞。阻止某件事情繼續發生，常用在新聞報導。也指靜止不動。和stop相似。

Unit 38 凸起

StringNet語料庫出現次數

bulge	protrude	emboss
334	224	61

bulge（vi.）

❖ 常用句型

S + bulge（+ adv.）（+ prep. + N）

❖ 例句

His briefcase was bulging with documents.
他的公事包裡文件多得鼓起來。
His eyes bulged in fury.
他的眼睛因憤怒而凸出。

❖ 常用搭配詞

（det.）n. + bulge
eyes, pockets, cheeks, forehead, walls, neck, face, shoulders, briefcase, veins, wardrobe, muscles, heart, file, skin, catalogues, bag, buttons, ground.

bulge with + n.

goodies, evidence, soap, documents, information, people, information, curiosity.

protrude（vi.）

❖ 常用句型

S + protrude（+ prep. + N）

❖ 例句

The dog slept with the tip of its tongue protruding.
這隻狗睡覺時舌尖吐出外露。

eyes protruding with excitement
眼睛因興奮而瞪大凸出

❖ 常用搭配詞

（det.）n. + protrude

tongue, eyes, lip, artery, arrow, rod, paper, head, hand, hair, arm, changes, feet, structure, pins, lever, limbs, jaw, tail, knuckle.

protrude + prep.

from, into, above, through, like, in, at, under, with.

emboss（vi.）

❖ 常用句型

S + emboss + with + N

❖ 例句

She was wearing silk stockings embossed with beads.
她穿著上面有珠子的絲質褲襪。

The name of the company is embossed on the invitation card.
這公司的名稱以凸印印在邀請卡上。

The knight's shield was embossed with gold.
這歧視的盾牌上有黃金浮雕。

embossed iron door
浮雕鐵門

❖ 常用搭配詞

emboss with + （det.）n.

gold, name, silver, beads, leaves, metal, gilt, scens, flowers, fruit.

綜合整理

bulge	因包含東西過多或太緊而形成的圓弧形凸出狀。
protrude	主要用在文章寫作，表示從某處伸出，通常是長條狀的物品，也可指眼球瞪大凸出，但較常指眼妝使眼睛看起來比較立體而明顯。
emboss	凸起的浮雕，例如紙張上燙金的字體或花樣。

bulge和protrude 都可表示眼球突出，另外pop也適用（例如His eyes popped out.），但pop的意思較廣，可以某物指凸出而脫落或突然出現，因此未列入此項目。

Unit 39 突然

StringNet語料庫出現次數

sudden	unexpected	abrupt
3701	2006	477

sudden（adj.）

❖ 片語

sudden infant death
嬰兒猝死
on a sudden impulse
一時心血來潮

❖ 常用搭配詞

sudden + n.

death, change, infant death, rush, changes, movement, thought, surge, increase, loss, silence, shock, burst, onset, rise, departure, attack, vision, flash, anger, fear, explosion, feeling, impulse, interest, halt, illness, decision, end, switch, collapse, realization, influx, pain, panic, arrival, noise, wave, flurry, gust, jerk, tension, drop, urge, sound, hope, move, spurt, desire, excitement, flood, fall, tears, heart, violence, transition, turn, introduction, realization, commotion, concern, reversal, release, chill, grin, leap, hush, lurch, revelation, flare, alarm, confusion, shift, roar, success, exclamation, exposure, upsurge, terror, darkness, cancellation, resignation, demise, stop, warmth, fame, outbreak, disappearance, flush, vehemence, power.

unexpected（adj.）

❖ 例句

She was shattered by the unexpected death of her son.
她兒子突然過世對她有如晴天霹靂。
The company failed to perform the contract because of an unexpected turn of events.
這公司因為突發事件而無法履行契約。

❖ 常用搭配詞

unexpected + n.

error, death, bonus, ways, results, victory, quarter, turn, places, things, success, visit, development, direction, problems, appearance, meeting, guest, finding, way, changes, result, decision, return, increase, invitation, arrival, source, announcement, event, place, visitors, difficulties, news, outcome, twist, rise, spin-off, boost, defeat, opportunity, effects, strength, movement, surge, support, suspense, resignation, kindness, consequence, attack, collapse, failure, move, situation, display, sound, delight, blow, gift, flash, wave, fall, encounter, shock, challenge, contingencies, power, degree, circumstances, praise, choice, response, light, presence, price, help, compliment, discovery, reaction, expense, illness, moments, cut, sight, noise, addition, windfall, caller, excitement, ferocity, depth, coda, glimpse, smile, appointment, tenderness, triumph, sensation, staff, contrast, behavior, items, suggestion, action, win, tears, dismay, trait, benefit, information, hazard, retort, departure.

abrupt（adj.）

❖ 例句

The meeting came to an abrupt end because of the accident.
這會議因為有意外發生而突然中斷。

The abrupt termination of Ben's political career was followed by his assassination.
Ben在他的政治生涯突然中斷後接著被刺殺。

He pushed her away with an abrupt movement.
他猛然把她推開。

❖ 常用搭配詞

abrupt + n.（pl.）

changes, transitions, disappearances, murmurs, addressed, lines, alterations, closures, questions, methods, shifts, contours.

one's abrupt + n.

departure, switch, change, entrance, tone, intrusion, disappearance, transfer, refusal, return, movement.

an abrupt + n.（sing.）

end, halt, change, stop, gesture, transition, rise, increase, conclusion, departure, finish, standstill, surge, turn, movement, swerve, shock, reversal, exclamation, onset, turnaround.

綜合整理

sudden	發生的速度很快，或者在沒有預料的情況下發生（例如sudden infant death）。
unexpected	在沒有預料的情況下發生，令人驚訝或措手不及（例如the unexpected death of her husband）。
abrupt	在沒有預料的情況下發生，也指唐突、魯莽的（例如one's abrupt tone）。

Unit 40 土壤，地上

StringNet語料庫出現次數

land	ground	floor	earth	soil	mud
21407	21000	11985	9205	4696	1863

land（n.）

❖ 例句

Judy's father works in the land registry office.
Judy的父親在土地註冊處工作。
The general died in no-man's land during the battle.
這位將軍在這場戰役中死在三不管地帶。

❖ 常用搭配詞

adj. + land

holy, promised, black, common, surrounding, new, same, agricultural, best, total, arable, central, national, adjoining, whole, chief, local, open, largest, lost, cultivated, remaining, derelict, necessary, great, salted, debatable, reclaimed, Irish, vacant, flat, high, poorest, extra, disputed, golden, industrial, fertile, right, lower, surplus, farmed, good, entire, available, major, Antarctic, dry, dead, occupied, drained, adjacent, main, Eurasian, barren, controversial, rough, residential, royal, unregistered, regional, joint, existing, vast, scenic, plowable, spare, terraced, virgin, grazing, additional, native, dominant, contaminated, noble.

land + n.

rover, use, reform, registry, registration, area, ownership, values, prices, act, management, tenure, charge, reclamation, drainage, rights, law, mass, surface, tax, supply, policy, sales, travel, agent, bank, availability, development, birds, forces, commission, acquisition, war, army, certificate, tribunal, animals, requirements, purchase, grant, transport, plants, settlement, cultivation, cover, degradation, areas, value, allocation, holdings, improvement, mammals, survey, quality, mine, securities, classification, market, cruise, resources, claim, speculators, clearance, fund, agents, raiders, revenue, provision, issue, disputes, transactions, border, routes, deals, rents, occupations, stock, compensation, boundaries, authority, drains, level, deeds, allotments, price, shortage, conservation, consolidation, defence, rehabilitation, inheritance, designation, legislation, affairs, surplus, surface, contamination.

ground（n.）

❖ 例句

Gorillas feed on ample vegetation found at ground level.

大猩猩的食物是許多種生長在地面的植物。

Her latest published book has broken new ground, providing new insight in social justice.

她最近出版的書開創新局面，為社會正義提出新的洞見。

❖ 常用搭配詞

adj. + ground

common, new, high, middle, open, cool, higher, rough, same, own, firm, soft, hard, stony, fertile, lost, solid, dangerous, level, flat, uneven, fast, lower, neutral, moral, little, low, dry, familiar, marshy, safer, shaky, rocky, above, heavy, bare, sufficient, boggy, white, hallowed, surrounding, consecrated, stronger, muddy, rising, feeding, dusty, sandy, sloping, fresh, holy, whole, basic, frozen, important, certain, swampy, disturbed, proving, moist, sole, easy, broken, suitable, made-up, derelict, allied, patterned, frosty, political, alternative, dark, central, damp, poor, green, arable, bumpy, American, major, steep, ideal, barren, soggy, rich, local, spare, soviet, undulating, unstable, icy, additional, ideological, forbidden, waterlogged, vibrational, secure, private, grassy, chief, cold, vacant, low-lying, contaminated, narrow, trampled, dense, slippery, sunbaked, well-trodden, entire, enclosed, rock-hard, ploughed, tacky, sacred, natural, shady, saturated, hilly.

n. + ground

county, breeding, home, football, recreation, training, cricket, burial, sports, waste, parade, manor, city, hunting, fishing, dumping, practice, school, testing, safety, hospital, road, center, battle, baseball, stamping, park, landing, university, memorial, cruising, college, welfare, display, council, house, church, killing.

floor（n.）

❖ 例句

There is a convenience store on the ground floor.
在一樓有一家便利商店。

❖ 常用搭配詞

adj. + floor

top, upper, wooden, tiled, concrete, each, polished, lower, mezzanine, solid, all, mosaic, main, whole, carpeted, hard, flagged, ceramic, sloping, earthen, bottom, extra, cold, white, bare, uneven, clean, wet, existing, entire, dusty, red-tiled, tessellated, dirty, single, level, large, flat, living-room, middle, total, marbled, filthy, crowded, stone-flagged, suspended, false, slippery, shiny, raised, additional, floating, original, vast, rough, rush-strewn, stalagmitic, open, paved, internal, basic, higher, proper, non-slip.

floor + n.

space, level, tiles, area, flat, boards, coverings, window, plan, manager, rooms, surface, joist, landing, balcony, show, leader, price, office, lamp, plate, bedroom, polish, accommodation, cushions, cleaning, workers, slab, apartment, extension, length, wax, exercises, cloth, elevators, edge, suite, wall, pattern, matting, limit, corridor, model, varnish, mop, traders, terrace, gallery, premises, sediments.

earth（n.）

❖ 例句

The aim of the campaign was to protect the earth's ozone layer.
這個活動的目標是保護地球的臭氧層。
the scorched earth policy
焦土政策。

❖ 常用搭配詞

adj. + earth

this, soft, whole, bare, brown, black, living, damp, new, red, solid, middle, beaten, wet, old, rare, moving, shared, entire, hard, frozen, baked, cold, spinning, total, chalky, natural, fresh, rotating, real, dry, dark, stationary, fired, wormer, dried, impassive, moist, rich, good, round, primitive, compacted, polluted, bloody, parched, excavated, virtual, green, surrounding, primeval, fragile, Paleolithic, hard-packed.

earth + n.

summit, science, mysteries, energy, commander, scientist, history, mother, spirit, movement, resources, report, light, color, system, floor, orbit, tremor, matter, surface, day, policy, peace, element, mound, clothing, satellite, metal, observation, rainforest.

soil（n.）

❖ 例句

Soil erosion is a serious problem in this region.
土壤侵蝕是這一帶地區嚴重的問題。
The rich soil soon became home to rampant weeds.
這片肥沃的土壤很快就雜草叢生。

❖ 常用搭配詞

adj. + soil

fertile, sandy, good, heavy, moist, poor, well-drained, British, dry, rich, top, wet, light, peaty, accelerated, alluvial, thin, contaminated, brown, foreign, damp, calcareous, organic, bare, deep, waterlogged, surrounding, shallow, local, black, volcanic, soft, chalky, alkaline, native, African, loose, particular, stony, free-draining, cold, rocky, national, compacted, acidic, ark, universal, stable, healthy, inorganic, natural, main, red, soluble, lighter, excessive, drained, gravelly, infertile, living, excavated, permeable, surplus, nutrient-poor, silty, bad, declining, muddy, tropical, leached, friable, lime-rich, frozen, adjustable, ploughed, sour, agricultural, saturated, effective, uncultivated.

soil + n.

erosion, conservation, structure, fertility, conditions, surface, degradation, loss, type, moisture, pipe, life, sample, water, science, profile, geography, stack, level, particles, properties, survey, acidification, temperature, formation, fauna, scientist, map, gas, mechanics, nutrient, texture, bacteria, quality, characteristics, flora, atmosphere, environment, system, compaction, factor, contamination, sampling, organisms, cover, deterioration, chemistry, resource, pests, removal, conditioner, protection, zone, analysis, damage, attachment, husbandry, layer, disturbance, test, background, solution, development, microbiology, movement, engineer, corrosion, studies, pollution, wash, improvement, crumb, sterilizers, exhaustion, manifolds, ecosystem.

mud（n.）

❖ 例句

The mud on his tires became the evidence of murder.
他車胎上的泥巴成為謀殺的證據。
A series of car tracks was seen clearly in the mud.
泥地上清晰可見一連串車子的輪胎印痕。

❖ 常用搭配詞

adj. + mud

wet, dried, black, liquid, more, thick, deep, grey, fine, red, glutinous, rutted, frozen, glorious, icy, brown, hard, packed, sun-dried, low, cracked, huge, contaminated, freezing, slimy, nude, glistening, bottom, artificial, organic, volcanic, bubbling, sticky, hot, baked.

mud + n.

flats, walls, huts, wagon, bricks, houses, building, bath, wedge, floor, volcanoes, bank, pies, patch, pool, wrestling, floor, road, stains, swelling, flap, nest, particle, tracks, shoal, circulation, cell, cake, sticks, complex, fever, heaps.

綜合整理

land	一塊地，尤其指農地或建築用地。也指地表的乾地，相對於天空（如land force地面部隊，land animals陸生動物）。也指國土。
ground	指地球表面的空地，也就是我們在戶外行走所踏的土地，包括水泥地。也指土壤從表面到地底下的範圍（例如dig the ground）。另外也指大型建築物周圍的場地（如hospital ground）。前面的形容詞許多是描述地形（如sandy, grassy, undulating等）。抽象意義表示理由、話題、或知識領域等（如moral ground）。在美式英語中指某種用途的場地（如hunting ground, fishing ground等）。相關成語有break new ground突破，common ground 共同點，middle ground 中間立場。
floor	室內或交通工具內的地板。前面的形容詞有許多是有關於地板的材質或狀態（如tiled, rush-strewn, slippery等）。片語on the factory floor表示基層工廠員工，相對於高層管理幹部。
earth	大寫Earth表示地球。指植物生長的土壤（=soil），地球的地表，相對於海洋和天空（=ground）。
soil	植物生長土壤的表面，前面的形容詞有許多是有關於土壤的成分或狀態（如muddy, lime-rich, acidic, shallow, compacted等），或是不同地理特色（如volcanic, tropical等）。
mud	濕泥巴地。前面的形容詞有許多是有關於泥巴的狀態（如wet,deep, bubbling等），或是不同地理特色（如volcanic等）。

Unit 41 土著的，土生土長的

StringNet語料庫出現次數

native	indigenous	aboriginal
2375	955	206

native（adj.）

❖ 例句

Her teacher is a native English speaker.
他的老師是英語母語人士。
The bird is native to Australia.
這種鳥的原生地在澳洲。

❖ 常用搭配詞

native + n.

speaker, language, land, peoples, country, tongue, species, tree, city, Americans, population, implementation, plant, Indian, town, village, tradition, Australia, habitat, inhabitants, bush, mode, woodland, Ireland, environment, forest, south, region, forest, authorities, liver, soil, tribes, pinewoods, heath, flora, stock, chief, dialect, fish, tongue, races, sources, community, leader, users, woods, animal, version, troops, plant, data, bird, style, climate, performance, protein, format, wit, wildlife, island, accent, support, breed, concepts, industry, caution, countryside, law, village, fauna, forces, vegetation, country, genius, life, habitats, area, custom, cultures, crystals, film, songs, code, biodiversity, music.

indigenous（adj.）

❖ 例句

The indigenous people were driven from their land.
這些原住民被趕出自己的土地。
to protect indigenous wildlife
保護本地野生生物

❖ 常用搭配詞

indigenous + n.

people, population, languages, communities, species, firms, culture, bourgeoisie, press, inhabitants, ideas, Indians, paraprofessionals, tribes, energy, leaders, workers, wildlife, coal, plants, concepts, traditions, industries, peasants, production, conceptions, organization, medicine, companies, area, businessmen, communication, entrepreneurs, breeds, majority, sector, demand, capitalism, issues, supplies, styles, designs, music, rights, art, meanings, theories, power, growth, cultivators, leadership, religions, women, land, classes, fauna, characteristics, reserves, bacteria, labor, folk, sources.

aboriginal（adj.）

❖ 例句

The origin of Australian aboriginal culture remains a mystery.
澳洲原住民文化的起源仍是個謎。
The material is widely used by the aboriginal inhabitants.
這種材料被當地土著居民廣泛使用。

❖ 常用搭配詞

aboriginal + n.

communities, people, art, health, affairs, land, societies, tribes, languages, culture, men, women, rights, deaths, studies, children, group, population, name, society, sites, life, word, inhabitants, concerns.

綜合整理

native	意義包含indigenous和aboriginal，此外並表示天生的（如native wit）以及原生的國家及語言。
indigenous	正式用字，某個地方土生土長的人或事物，相對於外來的，表示本地的，後面的名詞意義比aboriginal接的名詞較多樣化（如indigenous entrepreneur）。
aboriginal	正式用字，原本表示澳洲的原住民，後來意義擴大為某個地方或國家土生土長的人或動物，相似於indigenous。

Unit 42 推翻

StringNet語料庫出現次數

overturn	overthrow	topple
652	477	404

overturn（vt.）

❖ 常用句型

S + overturn + O

❖ 例句

The decision was overturned by the Supreme Court.
這個決定被最高法院推翻。
How can we overturn the habits of a life time？
我們如何能改變根深蒂固的習慣呢？

❖ 常用搭配詞

overturn the + n.

decision,ban, conviction, roe, settlement, result, veto, presumption, verdict, layer, disaster, ice cream, boat.

overthrow（vt.）

❖ 常用句型

S + overthrow + O

❖ 例句

They were plotting to overthrow the government.
他們策動陰謀要推翻政府。
The dynasty was overthrown and the country became a republic.
那王朝被推翻，然後這個國家變成共和國。

❖ 常用搭配詞

overthrow the + n.
government, system, monarchy, bourgeoisie, tsar, landlords, regime, state, republic, power, ledership, authorities.

topple（vi./vt.）

❖ 常用句型

S + topple + O
S + topple（+ adv.）

❖ 例句

The man lost his balance and started to topple backwards.
那個男子失去平衡，開始往後倒。
a military success in toppling the government
成功推翻政府的軍事行動。

❖ 常用搭配詞

topple the + n.
government, regime, gods, rest, heads, edifice.

綜合整理

overthrow	推翻領導人或政府的權力，特別指用暴力。
overturn	除了表示推翻領導人或政府的權力，也指把某個實體東西上下顛倒，另外也指推翻之前的決定或裁決。
topple	推翻領導人或政府的權力，不一定使用暴力。另外也指使堆高的東西不穩而致倒下。

Unit 43 通道，路線

StringNet語料庫出現次數

track	route	path	trail
7500	7489	7252	1388

track（n.）

❖ 例句

The police kept track of the movement of the drug dealer.
警方追蹤毒販的行動。
The hunter stopped in his tracks, noticing something in the wood.
那獵人半路停下，注意到樹林裡有動靜。
The construction of the cycle track system is a good news to cyclists.
腳踏車步道系統的興建對騎腳踏車的人是好消息。

❖ 常用搭配詞

n. + track

railway, title, dirt, copper, sound, cart, cycle, farm, rail, forest, tram, backing, data, mast, opening, curtain, gauge, grass, rhythm, cinder, perimeter, dance, album, outbound, road, forestry, guitar, twin, inbound, tyre, railroad, gravel, training, sheep, conduit, greyhound, mountain, overflow, test, animal, jungle, car, midlands, side, snail, park, steel, music.

route（n.）

❖ 例句

They are checking the escape route for a fire.
他們在檢查火災逃生路線。
He can't find any escape route from his trouble.
他對於他的困難找不到出路。

❖ 常用搭配詞

n. + route

escape, bus, trade, cycle, sea, town, migration, tram, supply, access, rail, road, coast, east-west, progression, mountain, transport, walking, palace, exit, tourist, land, trading, fuel, transmission, pilgrimage, railway, canal, packhorse, commuter, intercity, traffic, valley, ferry, return, trolleybus, shipping, communication, heath, disposal, patrol, motorway, silk, pedestrian, country, pilgrim, bike, cable, pass, tunnel, freight, career, entry, coach, street, investment, water, grade, circle, express, tanker, descent, circulation, ledge, desert, lowland, trolley, excursion, caravan, advertising.

path（n.）

❖ 例句

The software company provides a logical upgrade path for the users.
這軟體公司提供使用者合理的升級路徑。

The city's press beat a path to his door after the scandal broke out.
在這醜聞爆發後全市的媒體爭先恐後地跑到他家。

❖ 常用搭配詞

n. + path

garden, flight, coast, career, gravel, cliff, migration, upgrade, cycle, bridle, growth, woodland, forest, data, equilibrium, word, riverside, perimeter, tourist, glide, access, flux, distance, mountain,grass, development, field, zigzag, cinder, railway, church, dirt, pilton, paper, search, time, signal, energy, flare, stone, tow, brick, side, tarmac, ridge, back, cycle-pedestrian, directory, foot, transition, village, sheep, waterside.

trail（n.）

❖ 例句

On the campaign trail, the candidate did not hesitate to attack his opponents.
在他的拉票旅程中，這位候選人不忘攻擊他的對手。
The national park contains picnic sites,nature trails, and gift shops.
這國家公園中有野餐區，自然步道，和紀念品商店。

❖ 常用搭配詞

n. + trail

nature, campaign, audit, comeback, scent, vapor, heritage, discovery, town, tourist, woodland, forest, lolo, valley, acquisition, blood, victory, election, smoke, paper, title, treasure, recovery, championship, takeover.

綜合整理

track	狹窄、路面粗糙，非人工建造好的路徑，可以是許多人踩過而形成的路徑，強調走過後留下的痕跡。另外指運動場地跑道、火車的鐵軌、和音樂CD上的音軌（衍伸為一首歌曲）。
route	指從一個地點到另一個地點的路線，尤其指大眾運輸交通工具規劃好的既定路線，衍伸為達到某個目標或結果的方法或做法。
path	建造好的路徑或許多人踩過而形成的路徑，也指颱風、某人、或車輛前進的方向路線，特別強調可以讓人繼續前進的空間，因此也引申為達成某目標的計畫或一連串行動（如path to freedom），或指人生的旅程（例如Their paths crossed for a moment and then severed.他們的人生短暫交錯隨即各奔東西。）。現在也用來表示電腦裡面的軟體檔案路徑。
trail	指野外鄉間小路，也指人事物或特別是動物經過所留下的痕跡（如blood trail, a trail of devastation），另外也指特定人群會經過的路程，例如政治候選人拉票的行程或遊客走的路程，衍伸為欲達到某目標而做的一連串事情（如the winning trail）。

Unit 44 圖表

StringNet語料庫出現次數

table	figure	chart	diagram	graph
21784	27146	2580	1774	1399

table（n.）

❖ 例句

Table 5 shows the results of the survey.
表格五顯示調查的結果。

❖ 常用搭配詞

table of + n.

contents, origin, fees, data, results, exams, course, school, statistics, number, ranks, values, figures, points, entries, elements, frequency, examples, degree, statutes, authors, costs, transition, weights.

figure（n.）

❖ 例句

Let me show you some facts and figures that might interest you.
讓我給你看一些你可能會感興趣的事實和數字。

❖ 常用搭配詞

n. +（be）shown in figure [num.]

option, page, command, cycle, design, relationship, structure, image, filter, bridge, network, circuit, relation, computer, patient, temperature, system, outcome, example, distillation, information, curve, model, function.

chart（n.）

❖ 例句

He used a phoneme chart to teach the pronunciation of English vocabulary.
他用音位圖示來教英文單字發音。

❖ 常用搭配詞

the + n. chart

pop, bar, indie, flow, US, album, singles, organization, video, billboard, color, scoring, yardage, flip, control, oculist, reservations, phoneme, slip, wall, dance, let-down, progress, intarsia, birth, structure, approach, weather.

diagram（n.）

❖ 片語

the diagram of the cooling system
冷卻系統的結構圖

❖ 常用搭配詞

n. + diagram

circuit, block, flow, phase, pattern, tree, wiring, network, path, function, systems, line, structure, timing, layout, scale, profit, stereo, box, planning, matrix.

graph（n.）

❖ 例句

He drew a graph of his life from 0 to 50.
他把他零歲到五十歲的人生用圖形來表示。

❖ 常用搭配詞

n. + graph

bar, line, word, phoneme, time, photo, knowledge, probablily, 3D, sales, drawing, pie, search.

綜合整理

table	在書頁中橫向列出的數字或事項的表格。以文字和數字為主。
figure	書中有編號的圖形或圖解。另外也表示代表某數量的數字（如unemployment figure失業率）。
chart	以簡圖、數字等表示的資訊，或印有此種資訊的紙張，也指流行歌曲每週的排行榜以及航海圖。
diagram	指用來說明某事物的位置、形狀、或功能的圖示，如心臟等器官或飛機的結構圖。
graph	用來比較多個數據的線條圖形，如折線圖、直條圖等各種統計圖表。

Unit 45 通知

StringNet語料庫出現次數

inform	notify	apprise
5222	956	30

inform（vt.）

❖ 常用句型

S + inform somebody of/ about thing
S + inform something that +子句

❖ 例句

She is well informed about Israeli history.
她很熟悉以色列歷史。
We will keep you informed of our progress.
我們會通知你我們的進展。
They informed him of the visit of the mayor.
他們通知他市長來訪。

❖ 常用搭配詞

be + adv. informed

well, better, fully, not, reliably, proper, also, more, immediately, never, officially, badly, ill, clearly, further, adequately, poorly, credibly, finally, wrongly, politely, personally, later, always.

inform + the n.

police, House of Common, spirit, company, court, user, seller, publisher, council, reader, king, queen, secretary, authorities, office, committee, bank, person, people, patient, work, system, debate, staff, buyer, commission, parents, government, driver, lifespan, other, defence, contemnor, station, applicant, plaintiff, referee, minister, child, victim, prince, parties, electorate, partment, teaching, school, design jury, teacher, unit, USA, archbishop, defendant, president, author, auditor.

notify（vt.）

❖ 常用句型

S + notify somebody of something
S + notify somebody that + 子句

❖ 例句

The winner will be notified by phone.
優勝者會接到電話通知。
Incidence of infection in each country must be notified to the World Health Organization.
每個國家若有傳染病例必須通報世界衛生組織。

❖ 常用搭配詞

notify the + n.

police, company, society, authorities, government, seller, public, licensing, deparmtnet, landlord, tenant, parquet, court, paymaster, office, executive, vendor, practice, planning, secretary, programmer, exchange, member, registry, revenue, system, defendant, purchaser, other, speaker, party, user, applicant, client.

apprise（vt.）

❖ 常用句型

S + apprise somebody of something

❖ 例句

The general director is fully apprised of what is going on in the company.
這公司發生的事情都會全部告知總經理。

❖ 常用搭配詞

adv. + apprised
fully, better, right.

綜合整理

inform	正式用字，授予動詞（inform somebody of something），強調正式的通知，常用被動語態（例如be informed of/about something），中間常用副詞表示被通知的程度或頻率。因為是正式用字，後面的名詞時常是位階高的人（如the prince, the king, the archbishop等）。
notify	授予動詞（notify 人 of something），常用未來式被動語態（will be notified），後面常接被通知的管道（如by post, by phone等）
apprise	正式用字，很少用，也是授予動詞（apprise 人 of something）。

Unit 46 桶子

StringNet語料庫出現次數

barrel	bucket	tub	keg	pail
1401	1356	492	121	119

barrel（n.）

❖ 片語

100 million barrels of oil
一億桶石油

❖ 常用搭配詞

n. + barrel

gun, beer, biscuit, oak, wine, pork, tar, oil, metal, water, rain, whisky, fish, gallon, lens, bulk, brandy, steel, apple, cracker.

bucket（n.）

❖ 片語

buckets and spades for kids
兒童遊戲用的桶子和鏟子
a bucket of water
一桶水

❖ 常用搭配詞

n. + bucket

plastic, ice, home, rhino, slop, fire, water, record, coal, metal, waste, champagne, pig, sample, lead, food, hyachith, mop, leather, toilet, inspector, tin, latrine, feed, iron, rust, collecting, aluminium.

tub（n.）

❖ 片語

a tub of ice-cream

一桶冰淇淋

a wooden tub

一個木桶

❖ 常用搭配詞

n. + tub

bath, butter, plastic, cream, margarine, twin, dolly, water, stone, bran, patio, copper, ice-cream, rainwater, flower, tin, garden, marble.

keg（n.）

❖ 片語

a keg of brandy

一桶白蘭地

a keg of firework powder

一桶煙火粉末

❖ 常用搭配詞

n. + keg

beer, powder, ale, metal, gallon.

pail（n.）

❖ 片語

a pail of water

一桶水

to hoist the pail

提起（吊起）桶子

❖ 常用搭配詞

n. + pail

milk, totem.

綜合整理

bucket	無蓋，有一個圓弧把手的塑膠桶或鐵桶，用來裝水等液體。和pail一樣。也是液體容量單位名稱。
barrel	裝酒的圓弧形有蓋大桶，多半指木製桶，少數指金屬製桶。也是油的單位，等於159公升。也常指槍管。
tub	裝食物（如冰淇淋）的有蓋紙桶或塑膠桶a tub of ice cream，另外常指浴缸或浴盆。也是液體或食物容量單位名稱。
keg	基本上和barrel一樣指裝酒的圓弧形有蓋大桶，但較多指金屬製桶，尤其是裝二氧化碳等氣體或汽水等液體的密封金屬桶，外面接壓力計等儀表或管子。
pail	無蓋，有一個圓弧把手的塑膠桶或鐵桶，用來裝水等液體。和bucket一樣。

Unit 47 統治

StringNet語料庫出現次數

dominate	rule	govern	reign
4296	3987（v.），18420（n.）	2514	354（v.），1814（n.）

dominate（vi./vt.）

❖ 常用句型

S + dominate（+ O）

❖ 例句

Magnificent medieval cathedrals dominate the skylines of the city.
這城市充滿許多中世紀教堂的壯麗景象。

❖ 常用搭配詞

dominate the + n.

market, scene, world, game, proceedings, room, skyline, city, town, debate, landscape, country, area, opening, news, earth, headlines, lives, economy, stage, field, race, work, conversation, population, region, west, meeting, UK, politics, campaign, center, second-half, view, discussions, government, industry, book, history, minority, countryside, court, agenda, production, square, house, place, system, state, whole, day, north, activities, program, street, scenery, action, gene, curriculum, women, process, style, policy, practice, playground, remainder, story, institutions, show, approach, desktop, thought, continent, schedule, assembly, weather, cabinet, ranks, land, weekend.

dominated by + n.

members, men, trade, women, Germany, events, genes, work, west, dwarf, issues, protestants, fear, machines, capital, studies, Apple, landowner, subsistence, history, technology, London, conceptions, cars, delegates, language, businessmen, mountains, livestock, habit, representatives, games, consideration, liberals, males, changes, kinship, government, people, Marxism.

rule（vt.）

❖ 常用句型

S + rule + O

❖ 例句

The Socialists have ruled the country for the past four years.
過去四年這國家是由社會主義者執政。

❖ 常用搭配詞

be ruled by + n.

tyrants, men, politicians, others, communists, fears.

n. + be ruled by

country, life, Comoros, Salvador, house, society.

rule（n.）

❖ 片語

people living under Japanese rule
日本統治下的人民

❖ 常用搭配詞

adj. + rule

communist, British, Colonial, indirect, direct, military, different, formal, normal, civilian, one-party, procedural, presidential, Roman, national, English, rigid, Soviet, international, Japanese, constitutional, federal, informal, arbitrary, imperial, authoritarian, democratic, foreign, firm, Nazi, political, bloody, ultimate, despotic, Islamic, thirty-year, governing, one-man, non-legal, socialist, rigorous, temporary.

govern（vt.）

❖ 常用句型

S + govern + O.

❖ 片語

responses governed by impulse and emotions
衝動與激情下的反應
the laws governing the physical world
物理世界的定律

❖ 常用搭配詞

governed by + n.

rules, statute, section, considerations, article, equation, law, rule, principles, cost, God, community, market, legislation, norms, requirements, regulations, money.

n. + governed by

contract, situations, systems, process, sport, state, way, sale, activity, science, variable.

reign（vi.）

❖ 常用句型

S + reign

❖ 例句

David reigned over the country for 40 years.
大衛統治這個國家四十年。
The family reigned over the city's economy.
這個家族掌控這城市的經濟。
The bikini reigned supreme for over three decades.
比基尼獨領風騷超過三十年。

❖ 常用搭配詞

n. + reign

confusion, silence, peace, chaos, king, darkness, harmony, apathy.

reign（n.）

❖ 片語

during the reign of Elizabeth I
伊莉莎白一世女王統治時期
to begin a reign of terror
開始恐怖統治
the early years of Edward I's reign
愛德華一世統治的初期

❖ 常用搭配詞

n. + of one's reign
years, end, context, criticism, decade, parliament, part, middle, unrest, policy, turmoil, phase.

綜合整理

dominate	及物動詞或不及物動詞，表示支配，掌控的意思，不限於政治，主詞和受詞的意義多樣化。
rule	可當動詞和名詞。對一個國家及其人民的正式統治權，和govern相似。
govern	及物動詞或不及物動詞，指對一個國家制定法律、稅制等的統治權，和rule相似。另外也有支配、掌控的意思，主詞可能是某種規則或定律等，受詞可能是制度或活動等。
reign	可當動詞和名詞。通常是指君主政體的君王或女王的統治。當動詞時大多表示占優勢或支配，主詞可能是抽象名詞（如Silence reigned for several minutes in the room）。

Unit 48 痛苦

StringNet語料庫出現次數

pain	hurt	distress	misery
7013	4316（v.），217（n.）	1462	1270

agony	ache	pang	twinge
985	557（v.），269（n.）	242	139

pain（n.）

❖ 片語

be at pains to do something
竭力做某事
pain and grief of the family
家族的傷痛

❖ 常用搭配詞

the pain of + n.

loss, hell, love, adjustment, labor, imprisonment, bereavement, separation. divorce, life.

hurt（n.）

❖ 片語

the hurt of love
愛情的痛苦
I don’t want to hurt his feelings.
我不想傷害他的感情。

❖ 常用搭配詞

the hurt + prep.
in, of, to, inside.

the hurt of + n.
the whole world, leaving, being ignored, love, the last years, his having forgotten her family（ones’ Ving）.

distress（n.）

❖ 例句

He accepted the possibility with distress.
他悲痛地接受這個可能性。
The criticism caused considerable distress to the actress.
這個批評使這女演員非常痛苦。

❖ 常用搭配詞

adj. + distress

great, much, considerable, emotional, psychological, obvious, mental, acute, personal, deep, real, fetal, genuine, extreme, severe, immediate, human, short-term, terrible, unnecessary, immense, inner, present, evident, great, undue, exceptional, prolonged, avoidable, increasing, intense, resulting, obsessional, enormous, general, serious, grave, conscious.

v. + distress

cause, suffer, exhibit, show.

misery（n.）

❖ 例句

Her husband made her life a misery.
她的丈夫使她的生活很悲慘。
This novel depicts a girl's inequitable share of misery.
這部小說敘述一個女孩苦命悲慘的遭遇。

❖ 常用搭配詞

adj. + misery

personal, sheer, extreme, total, great, absolute, utter, real, prolonged, helpless, intense, deep, dull, individual, emotion, general, appalling.

misery of + n.

unemployment, people, women, humiliation, imprisonment, radiotherapy, bankruptcy, adolescence.

agony（n.）

❖ 片語

the agony of mind
心靈的傷痛
the agony of love
愛情的傷痛

❖ 常用搭配詞

an agony of + n.
apprehension, embarrassment, pleasure, suspense, frustration, lamentation, excitement, rapture.

adj. + agony
such, absolute, eternal, uncontrollable, horrifying, constant, excruciating, permanent, extreme.

ache（n.）

❖ 片語

an ache in one's heart
心中之痛

❖ 常用搭配詞

ache of +（det.）n.
loss, desire, love, hunger, loneliness, uncertainty, disappointment, separation.

pang（n.）

❖ 例句

He was seized by a pang of conscience.
他感到一陣良心不安。
He felt a pang of guilt.
他覺得有罪惡感。

❖ 常用搭配詞

a pang of + n.
jealousy, remorse, envy, gratitude, dismay, anxiety, pain, regret, grief, nostalgia, shame, sadness, disappointment, guilt.

with/feel a + adj. pang of
sharp, sudden, desolate, deep, tiny, little, immediate.

twinge（n.）

❖ 片語

to feel a twinge of sadness
感到一絲悲傷

❖ 常用搭配詞

a twinge of + n.

guilt, sadness, jealousy, envy, conscience, disappointment, regret, sympathy, pain, unease, discomfort, panic, uneasiness, anguish, nervousness.

綜合整理

此項目只探討精神上的痛苦	
pain	精神上的傷痛。此字有許多相關成語，如a pain in the neck指難對付或惹人厭的人或事。Be at pains to do something表示熱切或迫切地做某件事情。常用在片語the pain of + 名詞，該名詞多為抽象負面意義。
hurt	可數或不可數名詞。當名詞時多半表示情感的創痛（the hurt in one's heart），當及物動詞時後面受詞可以是主詞或別人，表示傷到自己或別人的情感（如hurt one's feelings）。
distress	不可數名詞。嚴重的精神痛苦，也指因為缺乏金錢或食物等引起的困境。
misery	可數或不可數名詞。嚴重的精神痛苦，如貧窮或病痛等造成的痛苦。
agony	指令人悲傷、困擾、不愉快的痛苦，如因為不明白、懸宕而產生的痛苦。如agony aunt指報章雜誌上專門供讀者投訴煩惱並予以解惑或建議的專欄。常用在an agony of + 名詞，此名詞大多表示負面情緒，但偶而也出現正面情緒。
ache	可數名詞。指精神上的傷痛（如an ache in one's heart，但也可以指疼痛）。
pang	指一陣突然精神上的苦痛，常用在片語a pang of +名詞，此名詞的意義多半是負面的情緒（例如regret）。
twinge	可數名詞。指一陣輕微不舒服的情緒，如罪惡感。

Unit 49 惱怒

StringNet語料庫出現次數

angry	furious	annoyed	outraged	irritated	incensed	infuriated
4024	1244	674	426	112	105	42

angry（adj.）

❖ 常用句型

S + be angry with somebody/ oneself
S + be angry about/ over something
S + be angry that + 子句

❖ 例句

She was angry with herself for having believed what the salesperson had said.
她很氣自己竟然相信推銷員的話。
The crowd were angry at the police brutality.
這些群衆對警察暴力感到氣憤。

❖ 常用搭配詞

angry + n.

face, voice, words, response, tears, reaction, eyes, man, crowd, protest, brigade, letters, scenes, look, mob, demonstrators, fans, glance, breath, parents, men, woman, retort, gesture, farmers, people, gaze, line, saves, frustration, demonstrations, sea, expression, resentment, silence, movement, feelings, group, surprise, meeting, residents, shouts, questions, glare, comments, debate, reply, wail, denunciation, murmurs, conversation, figure, reaction, outburst, attack, lion, bees, energy, moan, note, awareness, threat, scorn, tone, determination, refusal, thoughts, cries, tirade, frown, confrontation, despair, sea.

angry + prep.

with, about, at, over, for, to, in, by.

furious（adj.）

❖ 常用句型

S + be furious with somebody/ oneself
S + be furious at/ about + N
S + furious that + 子句

❖ 例句

They were furious with Johnny for bringing the police.

他們對於Johnny帶警察來大為光火。

The queen was furious at the scandal.

皇后對此醜聞表示震怒。

❖ 常用搭配詞

furious + n.

row, face, pace, reaction, argument, voice, expression, debate, look, rate, response, fight, letter, world, outburst, opposition, backlash, attack, eyes, rush, retort, barking, parents, rage, glare, glance, driving, denunciations, controversy, pretests, resentment, determination, gallop, gaze, storm, climate, onslaught, waves, residents, disbelief.

annoyed（adj.）

❖ 常用句型

S + be annoyed at/ with somebody
S + be annoyed about/ by something
S + be annoyed that + 子句

❖ 例句

We are pretty annoyed with him.
他使我們很苦惱。
He was annoyed at not being believed.
他因為不被相信感到苦惱。

❖ 常用搭配詞

be annoyed at the + n.

way, interruption, boldness, thought, lack, sight, behavior, exhibition, manipulation, outcome, trouble.

outraged（adj.）

❖ 常用句型

S + be outraged by + N

❖ 例句

Citizens are outraged by the soaring house prices.
人民對飆高的房價深感憤怒。

❖ 常用搭配詞

be outraged by +（the） n.

unjust crime, brutal assault, change, ruling, bloody repression, scale of corruption, suggestion, stagnation, treatment, excess, response, dismissal, way, performance, novel, murder, remark, fact, village gossips.

outraged + n.

public, expression, voice, protest, parents, pride, husband, residents, citizens.

irritated（adj.）

❖ 常用句型

S + irritated at/ about/ with/ by + N

❖ 例句

She was irritated with herself for feeling afraid.
她很氣自己感到害怕。

❖ 常用搭配詞

irritated by one's + n.

being there, slow pace, anxiety, disbelief, answer, manner, request, whining, questioning, coldness, intervention, interruption, refusal, presence, lack of fitness, forgetfulness.

infuriated（adj./vt.）

❖ 常用句型

S + be infuriated
S + infuriate + O

❖ 例句

He was more infuriated than wounded.
他被激怒的程度超過受傷的程度。

❖ 常用搭配詞

infuriated + n.

Charles（name）, followers, scientists, master, opponent, gentry, mob, wife, players.

incensed（adj.）

❖ 常用句型

S + be incensed at + N
S + be incensed that + 子句

❖ 例句

His neighbors were incensed at his arrogant attitude.
他的鄰居們被他高傲的態度氣極了。

❖ 常用搭配詞

（det.） n. + be incensed
he, she, taylor, people.

綜合整理

angry	最常見。指因別人的行為不當或不公平現象而生氣，和annoyed相似。
furious	極度生氣。
annoyed	較輕微的生氣，和irritated相似。後面不常接名詞，大多接介系詞如at/ with/ by/ about等或that子句。
outraged	極度生氣且震驚。後面介系詞最常接by。
irritated	較輕微的生氣，和annoyed相似。後面介系詞最常接by。
infuriated	極度生氣。後面介系詞最常接by。
incensed	極度生氣。後面介系詞最常接by。不可出現在名詞前面。
補充：以上形容詞大多由動詞衍生而來，如annoy, irritate, outrage, infuriate, incense，表示激怒，另外provoke除了引起的意義以外，也有激怒之意，特別強調故意挑釁，常用在固定片語provoke somebody into（doing）sth（如to provoke someone into a fight.）。	

Unit 50 能夠

StringNet語料庫出現次數

can	could	able	capable
261333	159607	29656	4822

can（modal v.）

❖ 常用句型

S + can + Vroot

❖ 例句

Doctors can detect the abnormal cells by carrying out a smear test.
醫生可以從抹片檢查找出異常的細胞。
He can't swim, can he？
他會游泳，可不是嗎？

could（modal v.）

❖ 常用句型

S + could + Vroot

❖ 例句

You could perform better.
你可以表現得更好。

able（adj.）

❖ 常用句型

S + be able to + Vroot

❖ 例句

He may not be able to afford the trip to Spain.
他可能無法負擔到西班牙旅行的費用。

❖ 常用搭配詞

be able to + v.

do, get, make, see, take, use, give, help, find, go, tell, offer, cope, say, provide, afford, put, work, keep, show, have, move, come, identify, buy, talk, look, produce, understand, read, claim, meet, pay, obtain, bring, carry, play, speak, hold, explain, run, continue, achieve, control, stand, handle, enjoy, write, sell, deal, maintain, live, think, draw, demonstrate, manage, respond, return, choose, compete, establish, support, turn, build, reach, develop, raise, spend, communicate, predict, accept, perform, stay, persuade, call, stop.

capable（adj.）

❖ 常用句型

S + be capable of doing something

❖ 例句

You don't know what he is capable of.
你不知道他有多麼厲害。
He is perfectly capable of passing the test.
他的能力要通過這個測驗綽綽有餘。

❖ 常用搭配詞

be capable of + Ving

doing, producing, making, carrying, taking, handling, giving, providing, supporting, running, dealing, holding, winning, delivering, performing, achieving, working, generating, causing, looking moving, using, getting, sustaining, creating, meeting, reaching, playing, detecting, competing, bearing, having, responding, beating, withstanding, expressing, yielding, coping, acting, leading, passing, forming, distinguishing, applying, storing, growing, operating, scoring, reproducing, understanding, accommodating, maintaining, exercising, driving, displaying, brining, keeping, living, defending, becoming, inflicting, existing, putting, increasing, revealing, supplying, standing, loving, destroying, writing, influencing, going, managing, inducing, rising, offering, setting, stimulating, converting, appreciating, identifying, explaining.

綜合整理

can	某人有能力做某件事情，也表示允許或建議，否定表示沒有能力、不應該、或不允許。
could	某人有能力做某件事情但是卻沒做到，也指在過去某個時候有能力做某件事情。是can的過去式。
able	be able to是正式用語，和can同樣表示某人有能力做某件事情，後面接的原形動詞意義廣泛。在情狀助動詞（如will, may, should等）和不定詞to之後只能用be able to而不能用can。
capable	be capable of表示具備做某件事情的能力或條件。Be capable of和be able to後面接的動詞有許多相同的字，但仍有些差異，be able to後面的動詞可表示身體器官的正常功能（如walk, see, hear等），比較強調做到某件事情的基本能力，而be capable of 則強調較高度的能力（如You don't know what he is capable of. 你不知道他的極限。此句暗示能力強大）。

Unit 51 能幹的

StringNet語料庫出現次數

able	capable	competent
29656	4822	1215

able（adj.）

❖ 例句

The university is trying to attract more able students across the globe.
這所大學嘗試吸引全球各地的資優生。

❖ 常用搭配詞

able + n.

pupils, seaman, children, men, students, women, individuals, assistance, program, member, engineer, work, teacher, staff, ruler, officer, lawyer, scientist, officials, minister, person, youngsters, assistant.

adv. + able

better, more, less, most, hardly, barely, least, always, scarcely, finally, quite, perfectly, reasonably, eventually, academically, generally, rarely, physically, apparently, equally, obviously, immediately, exceptionally, currently, necessarily, consequently, supposedly, sufficiently, gradually.

capable（adj.）

❖ 例句

He leaves the whole matter in your capable hands.
他把整件事情都交給你的巧手來處理。

❖ 常用搭配詞

capable + n.

hands, woman, people, finger, performer, manager, editor, staff, power, researcher, boy, child, officers, administrator.

competent（adj.）

❖ 例句

A competent teacher should be able to teach disobedient students.
一位稱職的老師應該有能力教導不聽話的學生。

❖ 常用搭配詞

competent + n.

people, staff, reader, body, man, minister, cell, practice, driver, hands, crew, teachers, amateur, adult, practitioner, student, professionals, mother, government.

adv. + competent

more, highly, less, most, extremely, perfectly, reasonably, fully, technically, socially, professionally, quite, equally, sufficiently, moderately, normally, supremely, clearly, fairly.

綜合整理

able	表示聰明能幹，最常接pupils。前面常接各樣的副詞說明程度。
capable	能幹的，能把事情做得很好，最常接hands，表示巧手。
competent	有基本能力做到令人滿意的程度，但是不是特別好，前面常接各樣的副詞說明程度。

Unit 52 扭轉，扭傷

StringNet語料庫出現次數

twist	wrench	sprain
1792	402	42

twist（vi./vt.）

❖ 常用句型

S + twist + O
S + twist（+ adv.）（+prep. + N）

❖ 例句

His mouth twisted with fury.
他的嘴巴因為憤怒而扭曲。
to twist one's ankle/wrist
扭傷腳踝/手腕

❖ 常用搭配詞

（det.）n. + twist

mouth, lips, face, smile, head, stomach, heart, fingers, road, arm, body, knife, hand, ankle, hair, shape, creature, paper, people, corpse, scarves, strip, driver.

twist with + n.

pain, rage, distaste, fury, bitterness, anger, arthritis.

twist +（det.）n.

knife, head, arm, ankle, mouth, body, wire, face, knee, ear, neck, hand, throttle, wheel, bag, truth, hair, nozzle.

wrench（vt.）

❖ 常用句型

S + wrench + O

❖ 例句

She wrenched her hand away from Cathy's.
她用力把手掙脫Cathy的手。
She wrenched his hand away.
她用力把他的手扭開。
He wrenched himself free of Evelyn.
他用力掙脫Evelyn.
He fell and wrenched his ankle.
他跌倒且扭傷了腳踝。

❖ 常用搭配詞

wrench one's + n.

arm, gaze, ankle, hand, shoulder, wrist, mouth, handbag, weapon.

sprain（vt.）

❖ 常用句型

S + sprain + O

❖ 片語

to sprain one's ankle
扭傷腳踝

❖ 常用搭配詞

sprain +（det.）n.
ankle, wrist, foot, back.

sprain（n.）

❖ 例句

Is it a sprain or a break？
是扭傷還是斷裂？
a left ankle sprain
左腳踝扭傷

❖ 常用搭配詞

a adj. + sprain
nasty, bad, suspected, severe.

綜合整理

twist	轉動身體部位、用手扭轉物體使彎曲變形、或扭傷身體關節。另外也指道路彎曲。
wrench	指突然、猛烈的扭轉，如搶奪物品或掙脫某人。也指扭傷身體關節。動詞wrench後面必須接副詞或介系詞（如wrench something from somebody），但是表示扭傷時不在此限。另外也指奮力（如wrench one's mind to the present）。
sprain	指扭傷身體關節，可當動詞或名詞。

Unit 53 黏住，堅守

StringNet語料庫出現次數

stick	adhere	glue
5762	789	486

stick（vi./vt.）

❖ 常用句型

S + stick something to/ on something
S + stick + prep. + N

❖ 例句

He has stuck with animals since he was young.
他從年輕時就和動物密不可分。
Some butter was stuck to the corner of his mouth.
他的嘴角沾到一些奶油。

❖ 常用搭配詞

（det.）n. + stick to +（det.）n.

grass/ grease, cloud/ sky, medal/ cover, marble/ floorboard, hand/ statue, tape/ machine base, tiles/ wall, flake /face, thread /wire, grave/ skin, petrol/ hair, skin/ metal, pancake/ ceiling, gum/ floor.

adhere（vi.）

❖ 常用句型

S + adhere + to something

❖ 例句

She adhered to her plan to study abroad.
她堅持出國留學的計畫。

The two pages adhered to each other.
這二頁黏在一起。

❖ 常用搭配詞

adv. + adhere to

strictly, always, still, rigidly, rarely, firmly, rigorously, stubbornly, actually, principally, properly, fully, usually, necessarily.

adhere to +（the）+ n.

principle, code, set, rules, timetable, road, church, faith, dictum, interpretation.

glue（vt.）

❖ 常用句型

S + glue + O together / prep. + N

❖ 例句

The gum was glued to her hair.
口香糖粘在她的頭髮上。
He kept his eyes glued to the young pretty girl.
他的眼光盯住那位年輕的美女。

❖ 常用搭配詞

glue to + the n.
screen, back, spot, television, wall, floor, saddle, roof, radio.

glue the + n.
fabric, sticks, frame, paper, flowers, ends.

綜合整理

stick	及物或不及物動詞。表示黏住或使黏住，也表示一直在一起不分離（stick with）或堅持（stick to）。
glue	及物動詞。用膠水黏住。也指因為專注而固定在某處。
adhere	正式用字。不及物動詞。表示緊緊黏住，但也常指堅守某種原則或規定等。字典的記載是不及物動詞，但語料庫有許多當作及物動詞的例子。

Unit 54 年代，時期

StringNet語料庫出現次數

period	age	era	epoch
28031	24517	2231	230

period（n.）

❖ 片語

over a long period of time
經過一段很長的時間
a film made over a twenty-year period
耗時二十年完成的電影

❖ 常用搭配詞

adj. + period

long, short, post-war, transitional, brief, inter-war, limited, earlier, modern, five-year, Medieval, fixed, postwar, initial, prolonged, Roman, interim, critical, historical, Colonial, intervening, classical, Victorian, current, probationary, Saxon, pre-war, deferred, Minoan, Anglo-Saxon, Hellenistic, comparable, Neolithic, present, glacial, equivalent, archaic, Edwardian, middle, temporary, preceding, Soviet, statutory, Romantic, revolutionary.

n. + period

transition, study, trial, war, consultation, Christmas, repayment, holiday, incubation, peak, interwar, gestation, training, grace, winter, loan, boom, treatment, planning, contract, honeymoon, sleep, rehabilitation, resting, evaluation, delay, recovery, trading, observation, adjustment, election, construction, opening, development, crisis, collection, registration, twelve-month, budget, retention, waiting, production, quarantine, recording, Renaissance, examination, classroom, migration, rotation, exposure, sales, lecture, monitoring, discussion, lunch, Baroque, sampling, learning, warranty, vacation, enlightenment, guarantee, suspension, childbearing, probation, preparation, Jurassic.

age（n.）

❖ 片語

in this day and age
在現代
for ages and ages
非常久的時間

❖ 常用搭配詞

n. + age

retirement, Bronze, Iron, school, Ice, pension, working, Stone, school-leaving, space, computer, childbearing, television, information, Jurassic, radiocarbon, breeding, machine, Triassic, Viking, Baroque, teen, adult, nursery, drinking, dinosaur.

adj. + age

old, middle, all, early, this, new, golden, median, pensionable, minimum, modern, school-leaving, gestational, tender, Victorian, retiring, advanced, bygone, nuclear, legal, advancing, Messianic, Hellenistic, military, Elizabethan, scientific, industrial, radiometric, technological, Augustan, mature, mechanical, atomic, electronic, successive, geological, classical, biological, terrestrial.

era（n.）

❖ 片語

in an era of world-wide recession
在全世界經濟衰退的時代
to mark the end of an era
為一個時代畫下句點

❖ 常用搭配詞

adj. + era

new, Victorian, post-war, modern, Edwardian, bygone, golden, previous, post-imperial, colonial, Christian, Nazi, Communist, Elizabethan, imperial, Roman, historical, progressive, classical, industrial, liberal, Mesozoic, Georgian, Romantic, contemporary, mid-Victorian.

n. + era

war, canal, depression, jet, jazz, steam, Baroque, boom, Punk, Puritan, liberation, hippy, pop.

epoch（n.）

❖ 片語

on the threshold of a new epoch
新紀元的開端
the end of a political epoch
一個政治時代的結束

❖ 常用搭配詞

adj. + epoch
historical, this, present, past, different, new, earlier, post-Stalinist, geological, progressive, feudal, previous, successive,

綜合整理

period	一個人一生中或人類歷史中的某個特殊時段。前面可接數字以表示確切時間長度（如a six year period）。
age	一個人一生中或人類歷史中的某個特殊時期（例如中年時期middle age或科技時代age of technology）。遠古時期多半以此字表示（如Ice age和Stone age）。
era	人類歷史中的某個時期，通常以某個事件或當時的特色為修飾語（例如hippy era和Jazz era）。
epoch	等於era，指人類歷史中的某個時期。

Unit 55 垃圾

StringNet語料庫出現次數

waste	rubbish	refuse	garbage	trash
5713	2029	273	272	182

waste（n.）

❖ 例句

The dumping of radioactive waste into the sea was banned in 1970.
西元1970年開始禁止傾倒放射性廢棄物在海洋裡。

❖ 常用搭配詞

adj. + waste

toxic, nuclear, radioactive, hazardous, industrial, domestic, solid, organic, chemical, clinical, high-level, low-level, agricultural, liquid, dangerous, urban, municipal, intermediate-level, poisonous, frozen, commercial, local, harmful, icy, recyclable, medical, tremendous, recycled, controlled, imported, existing, public, inert, decomposing, useless, barren, remaining, metabolic, biodegradable, marine.

waste + n.

disposal, management, ground, paper, products, water, pipe, material, collection, dump, yarn, bin, dumping, incinerator, regulation, matter, heat, recycling, sites, treatment, imports, minimization, outlet, incineration, problem, wood, producer, storage, repository, acid, inspectorate, transfer, reduction, container, oil, basket, generation, processing, control, agency, food, shipment, chain, timber, disposers, issue, packaging, collectors, contractor, glass, bucket, emissions, policy, avoidance, burial, energy, authority, transport, capacity, business, contamination, tires, ash, gas, metal.

rubbish（n.）

❖ 例句

Where is the best location to keep your rubbish bin in the living room without looking unclean？

把你的垃圾桶放在客廳哪裡才不會看起來髒亂？

After watching the movie, Tom considered it a load of rubbish.

看完這部電影，Tom認為它是一堆垃圾。

❖ 常用搭配詞

adj. + rubbish

household, garden, plastic, council, city, tons.

rubbish + n.

bin, tip, dump, disposal, skip, heap, collection, bag, pits, collectors, chute, manager, piles, trucks, industry.

refuse（n.）

❖ 例句

She is doing a study on the policies of refuse collection in several big cities.
她正在研究幾個大城市垃圾收集的政策。

❖ 常用搭配詞

adj. + refuse
domestic, uncollected, human, local, damp.

refuse + n.
collection, collectors, truck, disposal, sacks, dumps, department, site.

garbage（n.）

❖ 例句

It is hard to assess the It the number of garbage pickers in this city.
很難計算這個城市裡收垃圾工人的數量。
Where is the municipal garbage dump？
市立垃圾掩埋場在哪裡？

❖ 常用搭配詞

adj. + garbage
this, regurgitated, black, green.

garbage + n.
pickers, cans, collection, companies, dumps, bags, heaps, industry, bins, disposal, boats, firms, truck.

trash（n.）

❖ 例句

He takes out the trash for his wife every day.
他每天幫妻子把垃圾拿出去倒。

❖ 常用搭配詞

adj. + trash

white, this, confirmed, poor, alcoholic, Nazi.

trash + n.

can, culture, freak, hopper, terrorists, prog.

綜合整理

waste	使用後剩餘不用的廢棄物，前面常接廢棄物的來源（如household waste, industrial waste等）或性質（如toxic waste, radioactive waste等）。
rubbish	英式用字，表示不再需要而丟棄的物品，如食物、紙張等。另外也指自己認為沒用該丟棄的東西。
refuse	被丟棄的廢物，相當於英式的rubbish和美式的garbage, trash。
garbage	美式用字，表示被丟棄的原料，如空瓶、廢紙，廚餘等，相當於英式的rubbish。
trash	美式用字，表示被丟棄的廢物，如空瓶、廢紙等，相當於英式的rubbish。在語料庫有不少表示輕蔑的說法，如white trash表示貧窮、社會地位低下的白種人，而trailer trash則是指住在拖車的窮人。

Unit 56 累積

StringNet語料庫出現次數

collect	accumulate	cumulative	accrue	amass	hoard
7781	1150	703	532	248	150

collect（vi./vt.）

❖ 常用句型

S + collect + O

❖ 例句

They are collecting signatures for a petition.
他們在收集請願的簽名。

❖ 常用搭配詞

collect + n.

information, data, money, evidence, signatures, water, stamps, rents, taxes, food, debts, dust, samples, paintings, feedback, material, points, firewood, pictures, plants, works, specimens, coins, books, rainwater, contributions, antiques, lusterware, goods, rubbish, waste, rain, facts, subscription, messages, butterflies, leaves, shells, flowers, documents, stone, gold, fossils, seeds.

accumulate（vi./vt.）

❖ 常用句型

S + accumulate + O
S + accumulate（+ prep. +N）

❖ 片語

all the discontents that had accumulated after ten years together
經過十年後所累積的不滿

❖ 常用搭配詞

accumulate + n.

evidence, wealth, money, knowledge, capital, income, points, arrears, credits, expertise, assets, carbon, funds, cash, data, land.

n. + accumulate

evidence, debris, data, material, larvae, knowledge, sediment, capital, years, sediment, dirt, water, need, money, tendency, ash, wealth, stress, droppings, desire, deposits, deposits, acid, ice, arrears, gas, cells, fat, millage.

cumulative（adj.）

❖ 例句

All penalties are cumulative.
所有處罰都會累計。
the cumulative effect of too much stress
巨大壓力累積而成的影響

❖ 常用搭配詞

cumulative + n.

effect, total, result, impact, probability, supplement, density, frequency, amount, number, distribution, gastritis, knowledge, burden, hydrocarbon, increase, length, percentage, gas, volume, depreciation, experience, product, incidence.

accrue（vi./vt.）

❖ 常用句型

S + accrue + to/ from + N
S + accrue（+ prep. + N）

❖ 片語

social benefits that accrue from economic developments
經濟發展自然增生的社會福利

dividends which accrue to foreign investors
外國投資客增生的股息
wealth accruing to the treasury
國庫累積的財富

❖ 常用搭配詞

n. + accrue
benefits, profits, interest, advantage, gains, rights, losses, surplus, savings, charge, income, amount, value, rent, prestige,

accrue + prep.
to, from, in, on, at, for, after, during, by, over, between, through, since.

amass（vt.）

❖ 常用句型

S + amass + O

❖ 例句

He has amassed a considerable fortune over the past years.
在過去那些年他已經累積了可觀的財富。
knowledge which has been amassed over the past centuries
過去幾世紀累積的知識

❖ 常用搭配詞

amass a + n. of

fortune, collection, total, body.

amass + n.

wealth, information, debts, evidence,

hoard（vt.）

❖ 常用句型

S + hoard + O

❖ 例句

He has the habit of hoarding newspaper cuttings about the singers he likes.

他習慣收集他喜愛的歌手的剪報。

The protesters are hoarding foods.

示威抗議者在囤積食物。

❖ 常用搭配詞

hoard +（the） n.

food, wealth, gold, charge, goods, stocks, seeds, copper, wisdom, tablets, cuttings, things, memory, laughter, token, butt-ends, grain-harvest.

綜合整理

collect	當及物動詞或不及物動詞，表示從不同地方收集某物，受詞大多是有具體形質的物品。也表示數量逐漸增加、累積。語料庫中以及物動詞居多，常用在研究方法中的蒐集資料（to collect data）。
cumulative	動詞cumulate的意義和accumulate一樣，但是在StringNet沒出現，在BNC語料庫僅出現6次，而形容詞cumulative在StringNet則出現703次，表示此字形容詞比動詞還要常被使用。
accumulate	及物動詞，指一段時間內逐漸增加財物或知識。當不及物動詞時表示某物逐漸累積成為大量。
accrue	當及物動詞或不及物動詞。隨著時間的流逝自然增加，如利息等。
amass	及物動詞，指一段時間內逐漸增加財物或知識。
hoard	及物動詞，貯藏食物或金錢，尤其指沒必要的時候，而是為了樂趣或未來不時之需。在語料庫中要當名詞用。

Unit 57 牢固，牢靠，堅定

StringNet語料庫出現次數

strong	firm	solid	secure	stout
19157	3604	3400	1771	393

strong（adj.）

❖ 例句

He is writing a book on the keys to a strong relationship between husband and wife.
他在寫一本關於夫妻親密關係相處之道的書。

❖ 常用搭配詞

strong + n.

position, support, case, evidence, opposition, emphasis, links, argument, commitment, hand, arms, relationship, tradition, supporter, character, preference, belief, ties, bond, reason, advocate, squad, will, personality, presumption, version, resistance, conviction.

firm（adj.）

❖ 片語

take a firm grip on someone
緊抓住某人

❖ 常用搭配詞

a firm + n.

grip, favorite, belief, hold, hand, commitment, foundation, basis, base, line, decision, grasp, belief, supporter, promise, date, intention, footing, friend, voice, dough, stand, offer, control, conclusion, handshake, idea, surface, proposal, emphasis, diagnosis, texture, policy, recommendation, stance, advocate, conviction, place, pledge, statement, indication, sense, peace, mandate, bed, recognition, crust, assurance, step, tone.

v. + firm

hold, stand, become.

secure（adj.）

❖ 片語

a well-paid secure job
一份高薪穩定的工作

❖ 常用搭配詞

secure + n.

base, position, basis, job, employment, tenancy, income, prison, foundation, relationship, system, framework, source, grip, footing,

solid（adj.）

❖ 例句

The course is designed to give ESL beginners a solid foundation in English grammar.
這門課的目標是要幫英語第二語言學習者建立紮實的文法基礎。

❖ 常用搭配詞

solid + n.

base, foundation, performance, wall, state, floor, object, mass, block, line, core, basis, surface, platform, grounding, body, wood, background, lead, start, steel, gold, material, design, defence, barrier, understanding, form, reputation.

stout（adj.）

❖ 片語

a stout fence of new, wooden palisades
一道用新的木頭尖板條做成的堅固籬笆

❖ 常用搭配詞

stout + n.

stick, shoes, walking, defence, leg, timber, leather, spine, wall, fence, boots, stem.

綜合整理

strong	牢固不容易破壞（如strong arm），不容易屈服於逆境（如strong character），以及堅定的關係（如strong relationship）或立場（如strong opposition）。
firm	較多用於態度、關係、或立場的堅定，以及牢固的抓取動作。
secure	指穩當的處境或牢靠的地方或建築物。最常表示安全。
solid	表示材質堅固或純粹（如solid gold），後面的受詞表較多是實體物品；接抽象名詞時表示完整、連續、或牢靠的（如solid reputation）。
stout	指物品堅固牢靠，尤其是有厚度。也可以指人的身材矮胖結實。

Unit 58 欄杆

StringNet語料庫出現次數

railing	banister	balustrade	handrail
367	140	121	93

railing（n.）

❖ 例句

He leaned casually over the railings and drank some champagne.
他悠哉地靠著欄杆喝香檳。

❖ 常用搭配詞

n. + railing

iron, park, metal, church, balcony, chrome, deck, hand.

adj. + railing

wooden, rusted, black, high, spiked, wrought-iron, cast-iron, broken, tall, ornamental.

banister（n.）

❖ 例句

We heard a bedroom door opened upstairs and the faces of two little girls appeared over the banister.
我們聽到樓上臥室開門的聲音，然後樓梯的扶手欄杆中間出現二個小女孩的臉。

❖ 常用搭配詞

n. + banister
mahogany, stair.

adj. + banister
glided, broken, wrought-iron, interior.

balustrade（n.）

❖ 例句

They sat on the heavy stone balustrade of the terrace, swinging their legs while chatting delightedly with each other.
他們坐在露臺沉重的石製欄杆上，一邊晃著雙腿一邊開心地交談聊天。

❖ 常用搭配詞

n. + balustrade
stone, iron, roof, veranda, marble.

adj. + balustrade

wooden, wrought-iron, crumbling, elaborate, ornamental.

handrail（n.）

❖ 例句

There are handrails beside the toilet for the disabled people.
無障礙洗手間的馬桶邊有扶手欄杆。

❖ 常用搭配詞

n. + handrail

iron, steel, stair, mahogany.

adj. + handrail

wooden, firm, ranch-style.

綜合整理

railing	常用複數，一整排直立金屬條形成的欄杆，設在地板或樓梯的邊緣，可能在室外或室內。也指這種欄杆的其中一支金屬條。
banister	樓梯旁邊的扶手欄杆，由一排直立於地的木條及頂端一長條木柱組成，大多是木製。
balustrade	設在戶外橋邊或陽台的木製、石製、或金屬製的欄杆，防止人掉落。
handrail	釘在樓梯旁邊牆上的一長條鐵條或木條，供人上下樓梯時手扶。

Unit 59 懶惰，懶洋洋，慵懶

StringNet語料庫出現次數

lazy	idle	sluggish	languid	lethargic	indolent
806	608	243	148	104	49

lazy（adj.）

❖ 例句

Her roommate is too lazy to lift a finger to clean after herself.
她的室友懶惰得不肯動一根指頭清理她自己用過的東西。

❖ 常用搭配詞

lazy + n.

days, Sunday, eye, smile, bastard, week, people, man, voice, summer, slob, cook, grin, amusement, sod, way, mockery, hand, dog, pleasure, river, picnic, git, sensuality, cat, finger, drawl, movement, body, compilation, disposition, quality, start, gaze, exploration, slowness, bones, waters.

idle（adj.）

❖ 常用句型

S + V + idle

❖ 例句

The expensive equipment has been lying idle for years.
這昂貴的設備已經閒置了好多年。

❖ 常用搭配詞

v. + idle

lie, stand, remain, make, sit.

idle + n.

hands, curiosity, balances, man, time, chatter, gossip, threats, men, moment, thoughts, resources, speculation, boast, talk, speed, bastard, people, banter, dream, money, chit-chat, hours, fancies, minds, conversation, question, way, life, luxury, capacity.

sluggish（adj.）

❖ 例句

We felt sluggish and lethargic after lunch.
午餐之後我們感到懶洋洋的。

❖ 常用搭配詞

sluggish + n.

water, demand, sales, growth, stream, sea, traffic, start, progress, economy, oil, blood, performance, trading, trickle.

languid（adj.）

❖ 例句

She greeted him with a languid wave of hand.
她用一個慵懶的手勢向他打招呼。

❖ 常用搭配詞

a languid + n.
hand, man, voice, manner, eye, groove, wave, charm.

lethargic（adj.）

❖ 例句

The heat made us lethargic.
熱氣使得我們懶洋洋。
Time in this small village was lethargic.
時間在這個小鎮變得緩慢。
The participants were lethargic to the point of unconsciousness.
這些參與者昏昏欲睡，快要失去意識。

❖ 常用搭配詞

adj. + and lethargic
depressed, dull, heavy, humid.

indolent（adj.）

❖ 例句

These college students are indolent and frivolous.
這些大學生既好逸惡勞又輕佻。

❖ 常用搭配詞

indolent + n.
fashion, procrastination.

綜合整理

lazy	身體不想勞動或做事情不夠努力，和idle相似。也指使人變得慵懶的，常形容天氣或季節等外在環境。後面可以接人事物等名詞。
idle	懶惰，另外也指漫無目的或無根據的。後面可以接人事物等名詞。
sluggish	人的反應較平常遲緩，不想動的、懶散的。後面接的名詞很少是人；形容人的時候多半放在主詞。在語料庫大部分出現的句子多半用在形容河流等流動緩慢。
languid	文學用字，慵懶的、悠閒的、沒精神的，可以形容動作（如languid wave of hand）或時間（如a languid afternoon）。
lethargic	懶洋洋、無精打采的、想昏睡的，後面接的名詞很少是人；形容人的時候多半放在主詞。
indolent	懶散的、好逸惡勞的。後面接的名詞很少是人，形容人的時候多半放在主詞。
另外shiftless和unenterprising都指懶惰、沒志氣、沒有進取心的；lackadaisical也是指無精打采的，但在語料庫出現次數極少，因此在此不討論。	

Unit 60 浪潮，水花

StringNet語料庫出現次數

wave	tide	spray	surf	undulation
5694	2074	953	240	54

wave（n.）

❖ 例句

The explosion in the sea caused a tidal wave about 165 feet high.
這場海裡的爆炸造成165英尺高的海嘯。
Wave after wave of refugees swarmed into the country.
一波波難民潮湧向這個國家。

❖ 常用搭配詞

adj. + wave

new, tidal, great, fresh, big, huge, sudden, square, little, giant, quick, friendly, further, brief, strong, freak, large, slight, casual, cheery, slow, twenty-five-foot, massive, tiny, long, final, warm, welcome, recent, hasty.

n. + wave

shock, radio, sound, plane, pressure, pre-campaign, crime, breaking, ocean, standing, heat, brain, bow, strike, air, Atlantic, contraction, water, calcium, cine, t, assault, blast, stress, merger, sea, people, storm, alpha, electron, amplitude, earthquake, surface, reform, pounding, medium, gravity.

v. + the wave

ride, feel, rule, skim, hear, spread, represent, demonstrate, watch, follow, see.

tide（n.）

❖ 例句

He was swimming against the tide.

他逆著海浪游泳。

A rising tide of war-weariness occurred after the civil war had lasted for four years.

內戰持續了四年後厭戰潮流開始高漲。

❖ 常用搭配詞

adj. + tide

high, rising, low, incoming, falling, political, black, big, flowing, thermal, ebbing, full, alkaline, new, red, shifting, strong, economic, hot, swelling, irresistible, receding, main, warm, deep, general, changing, rushing, encroaching, vast, heavy, outing, current, mounting, conflicting, advancing.

n. + tide

spring, ebb, flood, student, night, battle, morning, ocean, evening, surge.

v. + the tide

stem, turn, catch, see, race, stop, ride.

spray（n.）

❖ 例句

There is a spray of blood on his face.
他的臉濺到血。
The hair styling spray is proven harmful to human body.
這種頭髮定型液被證實對人體有害。

❖ 常用搭配詞

adj. + spray

small, fine, chemical, protective, white, nasal, non-aerosol, red, natural, freezing, flying, light, adjustable, cold, specialized, facial, misty, wind-blown, concentrated, genetic, continuous, proprietary, vary, salty, stinging, gentle, separate, delicate, short.

n. + spray

salt, body, sea, water, fixing, styling, aerosol, hair, fly, paint, pumping, insect, gel, perfume, gold, curl, ocean, snow, forming, anesthetic, bug.

v. +（det.）spray

eject, minimize, watch, send, collect.

spray + n.

paint, bar, patterns, drift, container, arms, system, tank, nozzles, application, design, pressure, heads, attachment, bottle.

surf（n.）

❖ 例句

He works in a surf shop.
他在一個衝浪板商店工作。
All their concentration was on the great white wall of crashing surf.
所有的注意力都集中在那股巨浪上的白色高牆。

❖ 常用搭配詞

adj. + surf
heavy, white, Cornish, distant, booming, Hawaiian, grey, British.

surf + n.
shop, board, conditions, city, zone, capital, club, scoter.

n. + surf
breaking, ocean, pounding, Atlantic.

undulation（n.）

❖ 例句

They could not drive fast due to the undulation of the road.
因為路面起伏不平，他們無法開車開得很快。

❖ 常用搭配詞

undulation of +（det.） n.

medium, terrain, earth, fins, ambulance siren, road, figure.

adj. + undulation

acute, natural, regular, deep, gentle,

綜合整理

wave	可數名詞。海中的波浪，也指聲波或光波，另外也指突然大量的增加。
tide	潮汐，也指社會大衆的思潮。
spray	飛濺的小水滴，如汽車開過地面積水飛濺起的小水花或噴霧器噴出的噴液。另外也表示噴霧器。
surf	碎浪，尤其是衝擊岩石或海岸形成的白色浪花，在語料庫時常指可以衝浪的大浪或衝浪活動。
undulation	正式用字，指水面上的波動或小浪，也指地面的起伏。

Unit 61 浪費

StringNet語料庫出現次數

waste	lavish	squander
3104	432	200

waste（vt.）

❖ 常用句型

S + waste + 事/物 + on人/事/物
S + not waste time + Ving

❖ 例句

He is reluctant to waste money on potentially unwanted presents.
他很不情願把錢浪費在可能多餘的禮物。
Don't waste time arguing with her.
不要浪費時間和她辯論。

❖ 常用搭配詞

waste + n.

money, energy, police time, water, paper, resources, ground, incineration, space, pipes, products, materials, treatment, words, petrol, tips, yarn, reduction, effort, years, minimization, regulation, land, electricity, opportunities, fuel, dumps, days, things, food, assets.

lavish（vt.）

❖ 常用句型

S + lavish something on/ upon somebody
S + lavish somebody with something

❖ 例句

She was lavishing praise on her students.
她對她的學生過度稱讚。

❖ 常用搭配詞

lavish + n.
money, praise, care, rewards, time.

squander（vt.）

❖ 常用句型

S + squander something on somebody/ something

❖ 例句

He has squandered a gold opportunity to study abroad.
他浪費了一個出國留學的大好機會。
The money, which can improve the life of local people, should not be squandered on an unnecessary road.
這些錢可以用來改善當地居民的生活，不應該浪費在不必要的道路上。

❖ 常用搭配詞

squander +（det.）n.

money, opportunity, chance, fortune, resources, possession, energy, chance.

綜合整理

waste	浪費金錢、時間、力氣等。
lavish	給予某人事物過多的金錢、稱讚、或關愛。
squander	因為不看重而揮霍浪費金錢、時間、機會等。

Unit 62 浪費的

StringNet語料庫出現次數

extravagant	wasteful	prodigal	profligate
452	282	103	33

extravagant（adj.）

❖ 常用句型

S + be extravagant with + N

❖ 例句

Don't be extravagant with the wine.
不要喝太多酒。
He enjoyed an extravagant lifestyle after winning the lottery.
他中了樂透後過著奢華揮霍的日子。
He complained that his wife was extravagant and they could barely make the ends meet.
他抱怨他的妻子揮霍無度，使他們入不敷出。

❖ 常用搭配詞

extravagant + n.
lifestyle, spending, way, expenditure, celebrations, use, purchase, displays, quantities, girl.

wasteful（adj.）

❖ 常用句型

S + be wasteful of + n.

❖ 例句

wasteful duplication of the research
浪費的重複研究
The board considered the project to be wasteful of time and money.
董事會認為這個計畫浪費時間和金錢。

❖ 常用搭配詞

wasteful of + n.
time, memory, space, water.

wasteful + n.
duplication, use, power, ways, method, competition, employment, system, overlap, practice, expenditure.

prodigal（adj.）

❖ 片語

the story of the Prodigal Son
浪子回頭的故事

❖ 常用搭配詞

prodigal + n.
son, daughter, outpouring, life, exploitation.

profligate（adj.）

❖ 片語

a profligate use of water
浪費用水

❖ 常用搭配詞

profligate + n.
use, spending, lifestyle, government, waste.

綜合整理

extravagant	沒必要的奢侈浪費或超過能負擔的揮霍金錢。另外也指過分、過度的。語料庫中的例子大多數用來形容事物，很少形容人。
wasteful	浪費金錢、時間、力氣等。語料庫中的例子大多數用來形容事物，很少形容人。
prodigal	浪費金錢，不愛惜光陰。後面名詞可以是人（如prodigal son浪子）。
profligate	浪費金錢或資源。後面名詞不能是人。

	prodigal	extravagant	lavish	wasteful
浪費金錢或時間	+	+		+
豪華，所費不貲		+	+	
誇大不實，過度		+		
慷慨			+	

Unit 63 浪蕩的，放蕩的

StringNet語料庫出現次數

degenerate	dissolute	debauched	licentious
191	25	24（BNC）	21

degenerate（adj.）

❖ 例句

The Emperor was known as a degenerate debauchee.
那個君王被認為是墮落的浪蕩子。

❖ 常用搭配詞

degenerate + n.

art, form, interval, solution, state, version, pair, case, offshoot, image, debauchee.

dissolute（adj.）

❖ 例句

one's dissolute husband
某人放縱的丈夫

❖ 常用搭配詞

dissolute + n.

pursuits, figure, days, habit, existence, friends.

debauched（adj.）

❖ 片語

divorced and debauched actors
離婚放蕩的男演員

❖ 常用搭配詞

debauched + n.

image, desire, lifestyle, skills, aristocrats, world, emperor.

licentious（adj.）

❖ 片語

indulging in alcohol, licentious sex, and drugs
沉迷在酒精、亂性、和毒品

❖ 常用搭配詞

licentious + n.

friends, age, celebration, sex.

綜合整理

degenerate	正式用字。道德上令人無法接受的，不能用來形容人。
dissolute	過著不道德的生活，如酗酒和性氾濫。
debauched	正式用字。行為敗壞，不顧道德，如酗酒、吸毒、性氾濫等。
licentious	正式用字。主要指在性關係上的不道德與放蕩。

另外還有二個類似的單字，但是在語料庫無相關資料：

1.dissipated也是放蕩的意思，正式用字，指花太多時間在肉體享受上，如酗酒，當動詞表示消散和浪費。

2.profligate：正式用字。行為不顧道德，放蕩不羈。另外也指浪費財物。

Unit 64 冷酷無情的，殘忍的

StringNet語料庫出現次數

cruel	grim	brutal	stony	cold-blooded	flinty
1352	1040	718	314	118	28

cruel（adj.）

❖ 例句

He is never cruel to animals.
他從來不會殘害動物。
It is a cruel twist of fate.
那是命運殘酷的轉折。

❖ 常用搭配詞

cruel + n.

sports, blow, joke, man, irony, world, treatment, way, twist, eyes, mouth, smile, game, deception, winter, thing, death, fate, circumstances, sense, words, trick, methods, environment, finger, trade, tyrant, master, manner, sea, injustice, behavior, teasing, life, practice, parody, grip, killing, torture, punishment, humor, tax, truth, climate, kindness, treachery, act, lesson.

grim（adj.）

❖ 例句

You had to accept the grim reality.
你必須接受無情的現實。

He looks grim.
他看起來鬱鬱寡歡。

Things are looking grim.
事情的發展看來很不妙。

❖ 常用搭配詞

grim + n.

smile, reaper, expression, reality, satisfaction, picture, line, news, death, face, look, discovery, humor, warning, reminder, fate, legacy, silence, story, prospect, note, amusement, set, finding, wall, resolve, truth, vision, weather, statistics, life, harvest, future, situation, surroundings, frown, period, grin, memory, certainty, mood, state, business, voice, times, tone, scene, awareness, laughter, mask, glance, task, inevitability, fact.

brutal（adj.）

❖ 例句

Ten passengers were killed in a brutal random attack by a young man on the train.
有一個年輕人在火車上殘酷地濫殺無辜，造成十個乘客喪生。

❖ 常用搭配詞

brutal + adj.

murder, attack, assault, repression, suppression, violence, treatment, honesty, husband, truth, death, way, war, regime, man, killings, methods, rape, torture, state, behavior, exploitation, end, tyrant, world, aggression, police, crimes, competition, sport, beating, business, reign, clampdown, society, manner.

stony（adj.）

❖ 例句

His father stared at him in stony silence.
他的父親冷酷沉默地瞪著他。

❖ 常用搭配詞

stony + n.

silence, stare, look, eyes, face, glare, gaze.

cold-blooded（adj.）

❖ 例句

The cold-blooded murder of the infant shocked the villagers.
冷血的殺嬰案震驚了所有村民。

❖ 常用搭配詞

cold-blooded + n.

murder, animals, creatures, psychopath, killing, massacre, vertebrates, bastard, reptiles, way.

flinty（adj.）

❖ 例句

He had that flinty look in his eyes that told Edwards his stance was rigid.
他眼中冷峻的表情告訴Edwards他的立場很堅定。

❖ 常用搭配詞

flinty + n.

look, stare.

綜合整理

cruel	造成他人受苦或感到不快樂，也指刻意傷害人們或動物（如cruel sports表示鬥牛或鬥犬等會傷害到動物的競賽活動）。可以形容人。
grim	造成他人擔憂或感到不快樂，常用來形容表情（如grim smile）或事實（grim reality）。不宜用來形容人。另外也有堅定不屈的或陰森的意義，所以在語料庫出現的次數眾多。
brutal	冷酷殘暴，不顧別人感受，沒有同理心。可以形容人。最常用來形容謀殺（brutal murder）。
stony	不友善，沒有同情心，在語料庫中鮮少用來形容人。另外大多用來形容地面（如stony ground）。
cold-blooded	對別人的痛苦無法感同身受，沒有同情心，常用來形容動物（如cold-blooded creatures），也可以形容人。
flinty	文學用字。表示冰冷沒有感情的，不宜用來形容人。另外常用來形容地面，表示燧石似的或非常堅硬的（如flinty pebbles）。

Unit 65 冷淡，冷漠

StringNet語料庫出現次數

indifferent	detached	brittle	lukewarm	unconcerned	impassive
587	557	442	169	167	148

uninterested	unresponsive	apathetic	frigid	stolid	phlegmatic
138	101	97	97	61	51

indifferent（adj.）

❖ 常用句型

S + be indifferent to + O

❖ 例句

He seemed indifferent to the outcome of the examination.
他對檢查的結果似乎無動於衷。

❖ 常用搭配詞

indifferent to +（det.）n.

conditions, outcome, religion, slurs, public, water, others, shims, fate, results, behavior.

indifferent + n.

form, health, shrug, attitude, performance, start, season, result, world, service, look, man, work, spectators, public, weather, forces, product.

detached（adj.）

❖ 常用句型

S + be detached from + O

❖ 例句

She described the accident with a detached manner.
她以超然的態度描述那場意外。
She said that she now felt detached from her former boyfriend.
她說她對前任男友已經沒有感情了。

❖ 常用搭配詞

detached + n.
way, view, manner, attitude, interest, observer, voice, observation, examination, look, sense, impression, objectivity, outsider, eye, scrutiny.

brittle（adj.）

❖ 例句

He gave a brittle laugh.
他冷淡地笑了一下。

❖ 常用搭配詞

brittle + n.
laugh, voice, sound, smile.

lukewarm（adj.）

❖ 例句

The performance of the band received only a lukewarm response from the audience.
觀眾對這樂團的反應很冷淡。

❖ 常用搭配詞

lukewarm + n.
response, support, interest, endorsement, report, reaction, reception.

unconcerned（adj.）

❖ 常用句型

S + be unconcerned about + O

❖ 例句

The guests at the party were unconcerned about the absence of the host.
這些客人對主人的缺席毫不在意。

❖ 常用搭配詞

unconcerned + prep.
about, with, by, at.

v. + unconcerned

look, seem, appear, remain, act.

impassive (adj.)

❖ 例句

She was impressed with the refugee's impassive faces.
她對那位難民臉上木然的表情留下深刻的印象。

❖ 常用搭配詞

impassive + n.

face, expression, eyes, stare, gaze.

uninterested (adj.)

❖ 常用句型

S + be uninterested in + O

❖ 例句

The mayor's son is uninterested in politics.
這市長的兒子對政治沒興趣。

❖ 常用搭配詞

uninterested + n.

sniff, people, pressmen.

uninterested in +（det.）n.

politics, struggle, racing, hassle.

unresponsive（adj.）

❖ 常用句型

S + be unresponsive to + O

❖ 例句

The President is condemned as being unresponsive to public opinion.

這位總統被責備漠視社會大衆的意見。

❖ 常用搭配詞

unresponsive + n.

interest, changes, pain, bureaucracy, woman.

apathetic（adj.）

❖ 常用句型

S + be apathetic about + O

❖ 例句

Many young people are apathetic about the problems in their societies.

很多年輕人對他們社會的問題很無感。

❖ 常用搭配詞

apatheitc + n.

silence, state, atmosphere, manner.

frigid（adj.）

❖ 例句

She talked to her daughter-in-law in a frigid voice.
她用冷淡的聲音對她媳婦說話。

❖ 常用搭配詞

frigid + n.

exterior, tones, atmosphere, resentment.

stolid（adj.）

❖ 例句

He radiated a stolid air of calm.
他散發出一種冷漠沉靜的氛圍。

❖ 常用搭配詞

stolid + n.

fashion, figure, elder, sense, employer, stupidity.

phlegmatic（adj.）

❖ 例句

The British are usually considered phlegmatic, orderly, and systematic.
英國人通常被認為很淡定、中規中矩、有條有理的。

He observed the economic chaos in the country in a phlegmatic manner.
他冷眼旁觀這個國家的經濟亂象。

❖ 常用搭配詞

phlegmatic + n.
way, man, temperament, Londoner.

綜合整理

indifferent	不感興趣的。
detached	detach原本是分開的意思，detached表示超然的態度，沒有情感介入。
brittle	表示態度上冷淡不溫暖的。雖然在語料庫出現次數多，但是大部分是表示另外二個較常使用的意思：易碎的、脆弱的。
lukewarm	原本指食物或飲料溫度中庸，不冷不熱。在此表示不夠興奮、不夠感興趣。
unconcerned	感覺與自己無關而不擔憂也不感興趣。前面常接seem, appear等連綴動詞，後面不常接名詞。
impassive	沒有表現任何感情的，常用來形容表情，不宜用來形容人。
uninterested	不感興趣的。
unresponsive	沒反應的，不受影響的。
apathetic	不感興趣，也不想花力氣去改善。後面接的名詞很少是人。
frigid	文學用字，表示不友善、不仁慈的。另外表示女性性冷感的。
stolid	異於常人的對周遭情境沒反應或沒興趣，通常有貶意。
phlegmatic	淡定的，木然的，不易擔憂或興奮。

Unit 66 離開

StringNet語料庫出現次數

leave	abandon	depart
61538	4329	1351

leave（vi./vt.）

❖ 常用句型

S + leave + O
S + leave for + 地點

❖ 例句

She found a job immediately after leaving school.
她離開校園後馬上就找到工作了。
They left for Singapore yesterday.
他們昨天出發前往新加坡。

❖ 常用搭配詞

leave + n.

school, England（國家名稱）, London（地方名稱）, hospital, work, town, university, people, children, Sarah（人名）, politics.

abandon（vt.）

❖ 常用句和

S + abandon + O

❖ 例句

The captain ordered the crew to abandon ship.
船長命令水手們棄船。

❖ 常用搭配詞

abandon + the n.
car, land, vehicle, town, forest, city, aircraft, village, building.

depart（vi./vt.）

❖ 常用句型

S + depart（+ from/for）+ O

❖ 例句

The liner will depart from Eastbourne on May 25.
這班機將於五月25日離開伊斯坦堡。

❖ 常用搭配詞

（det.） n. + depart from

coach, trains, aircraft, guest, tour, girl, cruises.

綜合整理

leave	離開某個人或某個地方。後面受詞是人的時候也可表示關係的終止。
abandon	永久離開某個地方或交通工具，尤其是因為情勢造成不得不離（如棄船abandon the ship）。
depart	特別指啓程開始旅程，主詞時常是交通工具如車船或飛機。

Unit 67 理由

StringNet語料庫出現次數

reason	cause	excuse
28501	9695	2174

reason (n.)

❖ 例句

There is no reason why a son should inherit his family business.
要兒子繼承家庭事業是沒道理的。

I saw no reason to doubt his loyalty.
我沒理由懷疑他的忠誠。

There is no good reason for him to ask for a raise.
他沒有理由要求加薪。

❖ 常用搭配詞

adj. + reason

good, main, real, obvious, various, simple, political, major, possible, particular, apparent, important, practical, economic, special, wrong, sufficient, personal, legal, financial, principal, valid, technical, social, common, commercial, historical, medical, logical, sound, fundamental, compelling, strong, primary, specific, prime, chief, sole, human, legitimate, basic, ideological, inexplicable, pragmatic, environmental, theoretical, strategic, official, genuine, key, convincing, religious, related, understandable, powerful, ethical, tactical, domestic, single, obscure, single, general, humanitarian, professional, administrative, sentimental, stated, precise, adequate, plausible, scientific, exact, justifiable, complex, disciplinary, substantial, original, cogent, moral, immediate, full, initial, selfish, poor, proper, serious, natural, alleged, solid, normal, private, unspecified, intrinsic, negative, rational, trivial, probable.

v. + reason

have, give, find, see, provide, use, require, suggest, create, seek.

reason to + v.

believe, give, suppose, think, doubt, suspect, expect, fear, do, feel, assume, change, go, worry, stay, reject, look, celebrate, complain, offer, hope, question, avoid, accept, support, want, suggest, prefer, tell, maintain, talk, try, obey, argue, become, interfere, disagree.

cause（n.）

❖ 例句

Chronic constipation can be the underlying cause of cancer.
習慣性便祕可能是癌症的潛在病因。
The autopsy did not yield a cause of death.
這次遺體解剖並沒找出死因。

❖ 常用搭配詞

adj. + cause

good, main, major, common, natural, possible, underlying, real, worthy, important, reasonable, lost, immediate, likely, primary, prime, external, social, particular, single, physical, principal, basic, internal, contributory, chief, just, political, probable, direct, sufficient, specific, final, significant, matrimonial, frequent, potential, fundamental, environmental, worthwhile, criminal, proximate, obvious, leading, unknown, pricise, original, apparent, nation, various, radical, deeper, new, unrelated, organic, allied, conservative, actual, medical, psychological, alternative, popular, multiple, ultimate, genuine, personal, noble, formal, economic, unjust, material, hidden, related, short-term, ordinary, competing, rare, substantial, progressive, infective.

v. + cause

have, give, show, identify, confuse, disentangle, find, seek, demonstrate.

cause of + n.

death, action, crime, poverty, accidents, cancer, concern, unemployment, peace, inflation, ill-health, conflict, failure, problems, anemia, acid, friction, stress, morbidity, mortality, complaint, war, dissatisfaction, change, depression, violence, trouble, difficulty, behavior, disability, injury.

excuse（n.）

❖ 例句

She made an excuse to leave early.

她找個藉口提早離開。

The express company did not have a reasonable excuse for the late delivery.

這快遞公司無法提出這次送貨延遲的正當理由。

❖ 常用搭配詞

adj. + excuse

good, perfect, convenient, lawful, legitimate, feeble, poor, valid, flimsy, lame, plausible, standard, possible, useful, adequate, old, pathetic, usual, slightest, real, moral, official, justifiable.

v. + an excuse

have, make, find, get, provide, need, want, offer, invent.

綜合整理

reason	某人決定做某件事情的理由，或某件事情發生的起因或解釋。常和個人意志有關，常在後面接to + 意志或情感動詞（如doubt, believe, suspect, fear等），動詞的意義可能是正面（to celebrate）或負面（to doubt）。另外也表示理性。
cause	造成某件事情發生的人事物。常和外在發生事件有關，常在後面接of + 負面意義現象名詞（如death, conflict, war, crime等）。
excuse	用來解釋某件粗心或無禮的事情的理由，也可以指為自己的行為捏造的藉口。

Unit 68 禮貌，禮節

StringNet語料庫出現次數

manners	courtesy	politeness	etiquette	civility	gentility
6578	1084	232	190	85	63

manners（n.）

❖ 例句

They were amazed at the child's impeccable table manners.
他們對這孩子無懈可擊的餐桌禮儀感到十分驚奇。

❖ 常用搭配詞

n. + manners

table, road, world, country, telephone, bedroom.

adj. + manners

bad, impeccable, nice, perfect, charming, social, excellent, gentle, aristocratic, courteous, formal, graceful, rude, courtly, polished.

courtesy（n.）

❖ 例句

The committee members exchanged courtesies before the meeting started.
委員會的成員在會議開始前彼此問候。

❖ 常用搭配詞

adj + courtesy

common, exaggerated, grave, old-fashioned, normal, great, utmost, unfailing, natural, possible, formal, habitual, mere, initial, immense, scant, final, characteristic, greatest, professional, usual.

courtesy + n.

call, visit, title, car, bus, light, taxi, coaches, ensigns, gesture.

politeness（n.）

❖ 例句

She is not accustomed to the stiff and formal politeness in the palace.
她不適應宮廷中僵硬表面的禮數。

❖ 常用搭配詞

n. + of politeness

veneer, absence, rules, principles, level.

adj. + politeness

social, natural, exaggerated, excessive, positive, old-fashioned, formal, common, conventional, wary, cool, studied, automatic.

etiquette（n.）

❖ 例句

The royal family apologized for the breach of etiquette.
皇家為了這次違反禮節而道歉。

❖ 常用搭配詞

adj. + etiquette
social, professional, strict, rigid, useful.

n. + of etiquette
rules, breach, book, matter, code, principles, stickler, points, lack.

n. + etiquette
court, restaurant, party, golf.

civility（n.）

❖ 例句

They behaved with great civility at the royal party.
他們在皇室派對行禮如儀。
He bemoaned the decline of English civility.
他哀悼英國禮節的式微。

❖ 常用搭配詞

adj. + civility

English, great, detailed, unheard-of, hollow, distant.

n. + of civility

veneer, march, skills, mask.

gentility（n.）

❖ 例句

The prince danced with discreet gentility.
那王子溫文儒雅地跳著舞。

❖ 常用搭配詞

adj. + gentility

discreet, suburban, petty-bourgeois, British, comfortless, slithery.

n. + of gentility

culture, concept, tread.

綜合整理

manner	常用複數，在社交場合符合禮貌的態度和行為方式。另外也表示某件事情進行的方式或方法。中性名詞，前面有可能接正面（如impeccable, perfect等）或負面意義的形容詞（如bad, rude等）。
courtesy	不可數名詞，表示禮貌、敬意，如courtesy call是外交官的禮貌性拜會。也可當可數名詞表示客套話。另外也指基於禮貌或善意而提供的事物，如courtesy car是車子維修時廠商提供的代步車。前面有可能接負面意義的形容詞（如exaggerated等）。
politeness	在社交場合表示體貼尊敬的說話及行為舉止。前面有可能接負面意義的形容詞（如exaggerated, effusive等）。
etiquette	某一群人或某個社會中的正式禮數規範。
civility	不可數名詞。正式用字。大多數人認可的禮貌行為。前面有可能接負面意義的形容詞（如hollow, distant等）。
gentility	正式用字。上流社會的禮貌、斯文、優雅特質。前面有可能接負面意義的形容詞（如comfortless, slithery等）。

以上名詞皆表示禮貌或禮節，其中manner是中性名詞，前面接負面意義的形容詞常表示沒有禮貌或態度不佳；etiquette則表示既定的禮數規範，前面不常接負面意義的形容詞；其他的名詞表示個人展現的禮貌風度，前面接負面意義的形容詞時常表示過度誇張（如exaggerated）或禮節本身的負面意義（如hollow, comfortless）。

Unit 69 禮物

StringNet語料庫出現次數

present	gift	offering
7687	4483	1310

present（n.）

❖ 例句

He received a lot of Christmas presents.
他收到許多聖誕禮物。

❖ 常用搭配詞

n. + present

wedding, Christmas, birthday, leaving, family, group, woman, farewell, member, engagement, parting, opening, retirement, graduation, anniversary.

adj. + n.

little, small, nice, special, expensive, lovely, perfect, big, ideal, good, new, lavish, generous, last-minute, marvelous, magnificent, wonderful, mass, valuable, disposable, suitable, decent, sensible, handsome, beautiful, practical, acceptable, simple, typical, unusual.

gift（n.）

❖ 例句

He gave his staff gift vouchers for Christmas.
他給員工禮券作為聖誕禮物。

❖ 常用搭配詞

gift + n.

shop, aid, vouchers, list, wrap, exchange, tokens, boxes, catalogue, tags, wrapping, pack, set, items, guide, mine, trade, taxes, donation, idea, business, service, time, cards.

adj. + gift

free, small, special, greatest, generous, precious, personal, wonderful, perfect, royal, particular, priceless, expensive, unique, ideal, charitable, unusual, real, unexpected, monetary, substantial, various, gracious, festive, unconditional, useful, artistic, rich, exception, annual, lavish, private, promotional, ultimate, outstanding, magnificent, appropriate, single, promised, traditional, marvelous, large, direct, suitable, token, financial, extraordinary, enormous, diplomatic, imperfect, God-given, lovely, evangelistic, valuable, conditional, creative, desirable, anonymous, elegant, edible, voluntary, political, costly, seasonal.

offering（n.）

❖ 片語

the sin offering
贖罪祭

❖ 常用搭配詞

adj. + offering

public, latest, burnt, votive, musical, sacrificial, initial, high-end, weekly, current, small, proprietary, future, competing, existing, fine, conventional, ritual, alternative, generous, various, private, planned.

綜合整理

present	為某種場合或表示謝意所送的禮物，和gift相似。因為當名詞另外也表示目前，現在，所以在語料庫出現次數較多。
gift	送人的禮物，表達謝意、喜愛之意、或為某種場合。和present相似，但是販售的禮品通常用gift而不用present，後面常接名詞表示禮品相關的事物（如gift shop, gift service等）。店家給的禮品也用此字（如free gift, opening gift）。當名詞也表示天賦（上天給的禮物）。
offering	給上帝、神明獻祭的禮物，或為了取悅人而送的禮物。另外當名詞也表示提供，或書本、戲劇等最新成品。

Unit 70 力量

StringNet語料庫出現次數

power	force	strength
37686	24548	8019

power（n.）

❖ 例句

The purchasing power of the middle class has fallen dramatically due to the continuous inflation in the past decades.
由於過去幾十年持續的通貨膨脹，中產階級的購買能力已經大幅降低。

❖ 常用搭配詞

power of + n.

attorney, arrest, God, veto, love, concentration, observation, control, persuasion, speech, reason, patronage, sale, trade, entry, nature, government, darkness, Europe, investigation, television, life, resistance, music, women, chaos, words, money, dreams, decision, intervention, invention, Parliament, enforcement, review, expression, flight, detention, search, coercion, recovery, description, discrimination, imagination, ideas, Jesus, endurance, disposal, choice, suggestion, sin, language, evil, individuals, prayer, water, expulsion, advertising, light, destruction, thought, leadership, courts, influence, magic, economics, market, bureaucracy, regulation, photography, death, parent, public, punishment, ministers, computer, seizure, passion.

adj. + power

nuclear, political, economic, national, real, legislative, full, coal-fired, military, discretionary, electric, royal, considerable, personal, solar, managerial, statutory, social, absolute, presidential, corporate, imperial, internal, popular, male, less, explanatory, effective, higher, black, public, sovereign, general, creative, local, foreign, legal, increasing, governmental, central, predictive, executive, destructive, divine, financial, ultimate, healing, supreme, arbitrary, tidal, judicial, generating, coercive, French, unequal, physical, temporal, inherent, civil, international, emotional, mystical, religious, dominant, human, administrative, redundant, dynamic, superior, symbolic, sexual, legitimate, ample, global, traditional, communist, sheer, negative, substantial, supernatural, outside, usurped, intellectual, domestic, cultural, suspending, ecclesiastical, causal, medical, western, evil, penetrating, uninterruptible, hidden, leading, striking, countervailing, current, parental, productive, autocratic, moral, rival, punching, emotive, cosmic, clean, muscular, constant, masculine, inexorable, malignant, declining, concentrated, Catholic, unlimited, unrestrained, armed, revolutionary.

n. + power

purchasing, executive, state, bargaining, labor, monopoly, wind, market, motive, union, staying, water, spending, computing, world, processing, buying, decision-making, community, engine, muscle, will, police, battery, people, voting, parent, veto, prerogative, consumer, brain, expert, government, electricity, stereo, management, sea, drive, court, lifting, student, word, law, man, borrowing, cleaning, media, occult.

force（n.）

❖ 例句

The scandal has severely damaged the image of the Royal Air Forces.
這個醜聞重創了皇家空軍的形象。

The President has announced the dispatch of the task force, which consists of 100 men.
總統宣布派遣為數一百人的特遣部隊。

❖ 常用搭配詞

adj. + force

armed, driving, political, military, full, nuclear, British, allied, conventional, social, democratic, Soviet, Iraqi, economic, powerful, naval, major, gravitational, productive, main, expeditionary, external, rebel, peacekeeping, physical, multinational, natural, dominant, conservative, progressive, reserve, sheer, dynamic, occupying, opposing, reasonable, strategic, international, electromagnetic, tidal, magnetic, motivating, combined, foreign, evil, irresistible, vital, hostile, negative, potent, local, weak, equal, centrifugal, regular, destructive, attractive, legal, attacking, superior, revolutionary, leading, competitive, creative, spiritual, supernatural, binding, popular, Christian, cultural, active, illocutionary, dark, invading, cohesive, selective, repulsive, unifying, countervailing, historical, electrical, unlawful, religious, joint, guiding, mobile, fundamental, cosmic, federal, statutory, unseen, intellectual, applied, lethal, aggressive, invisible, independent, frictional, formidable, emotional, global.

n. + force

air, police, security, labor, task, market, work, defence, sales, government, US, UN, life, brute, ground, teaching, opposition, fighting, protection, strike, coalition, reaction, volunteer, commodore, invasion, support, pathfinder, land, guerrilla, enemy, NATO, motive, cadet, commonwealth, assault, class, deployment, occupation, liberation, storm, combat, peace, field, body, resistance, army, reform, intervention, bomber, chaos, pact, nations, mobile, buoyancy, healing, action, relief, state, impact.

strength（n.）

❖ 例句

He gained strength after resting for two months.
休息二個月後他恢復了體力。

❖ 常用搭配詞

strength of + n.

character, feeling, will, mind, purpose, opposition, personality, sterling, God, materials, Gloucester, partisanship, demand, trade, wood, support, nationalism, labor, Germany, selection, gold, timber, steel, co-operation, color, gender, solution, recession, network, comments, pubic, union, tendons, love, desperation.

n. + of strength

tower, position, source, show, trial, reserves, areas, test, sort, lack, feats, display, well, loss, level, sign, potion, surge.

adj. + strength

great, full, physical, relative, military, competitive, economic, inner, tensile, financial, real, associative, growing, political, mechanical, considerable, high, superior, industrial, underlying, major, spiritual, current, personal, numerical, continuing, individual, electoral, alcoholic, muscular, traditional, collective, increasing, equal, transcriptional, sheer, moral, ultimate, academic, commercial, hidden, all-round, desired, inherent, overwhelming, effective, superhuman, practical, mental, emotional, perceived, solid, social, parliamentary, respective, natural, double, supernatural, characteristic, national, key, unusual, divine, conventional, compelling, innate, gentle.

n. + strength

field, strength, wind, brute, network, voting, union, business, research, negotiating, party, signal, police, muscle, impact, troop, guerrilla, bond, marketing, manufacturing, line, brand, hair, body, ration, odor, steel.

綜合整理

power	1.掌控、影響人群或事情的能力或權利。2.政府等組織的權力。3.物理力量或影響力。4.電力。
force	1.武裝部隊（常用複數）、軍事行動、或武力。2.移動或撞擊的力量（和strength相似）。3.大自然的力量（如natural force, the force of nature）。4.動員人力（如sales force, task force等）。5.驅動力或驅動者（driving force）。本身具有多種意義，因此前面時常接名詞或形容詞以釐清意義，語料庫沒有有force of + 名詞的句型。
strength	1.人的體力或心志的力量。2.一個國家或組織的政治經濟或軍事力量（如show of strength）。3.實體物件的堅固程度（耐力）。4.人的優點。

power和strength前面有不少相同的搭配詞，但是意義不一定相同，如economic power 和 economic strength雖然在語料庫都有出現，但前者次數高出許多（economic power出現200次，economic strength則是43次）.，表示經濟實力及影響力，後者則指（國家）擁有的財力。political power是指行政權力，而political（party）strength則是某個政黨的政治實力。Military power可以指一個國家的軍隊或軍事強國，而military strength則是一個國家的整體軍事力量。

Unit 71 立場、態度

StringNet語料庫出現次數

position	attitude	stance
26209	10507	1814

position（n.）

❖ 常用句型

S + take the position that + 子句
S + make one's position clear on + N

❖ 例句

What's the party's position on death penalty？
這個政黨對於死刑的立場如何？
The President has not made his position clear on the proposal.
對於這個提案總統尚未表明立場。

❖ 常用搭配詞

n.'s + position

government, women, party, Britain, council, Gloucester, UK, church, client, father, Japan, London, company, labor, minister, family, Thatcher, opposition, opponent.

adj. + position

present, social, original, current, economic, competitive, political, correct, defensive, unique, initial, official, theoretical, international, extreme, ideological, previous, various, normal, intermediate, responsible, public, personal, unusual, moral, basic, conservative, invidious, British, critical, changing, rightful, suitable, entrenched, neutral, Christian, theological, wrong, ambiguous, identical, earlier, approximate, doctrinal, religious, radical, proper, curious, ethical, liberal, contradictory, crucial, western, bad, conspicuous, definite, perilous, mean, consistent, absolute, reasonable, diplomatic, opposite, significant, academic, intransigent, anti-cruelty, ridiculous, feminist, varying, underlying, firm, judicial.

attitude（n.）

❖ 例句

He held a skeptical attitude toward the new treatment.
他對於新的治療法抱持懷疑。

❖ 常用搭配詞

adj. + attitude

positive, different, negative, right, general, ambivalent, critical, public, aggressive, British, responsible, professional, cavalier, liberal, favorable, wrong, prevailing, sympathetic, skeptical, cautious, dismissive, caring, political, changed, uncompromising, reasonable, open, current, changing, common, laid-back, patronizing, complacent, question, dictatorial, passive, conciliatory, neutral, friendly, protective, Christian, French, healthy, correct, tolerant, tradition, bad, parental, objective, basic, permissive, mature, emotional, pragmatic, proper, happy-go-lucky, detached, irreverent, western, sensible, underlying, competitive, social, paternalistic, conservative, scientific, good, cynical, belligerent, defensive, flexible, poor, serious, devil-may-care, moral, down-to-earth, ambiguous, natural, effective, rebellious, interpretive, normal, cooperative, holistic, stupid, national, definite, disdainful, mean, tough, single-minded, judicial, throw-away, straightforward, realistic, pioneering, disparaging, weird, stern.

v. + a + adj. + attitude

have, adopt, take, maintain, imply.

stance（n.）

❖ 例句

The President adopted an anti-abortion stance.

總統對墮胎持反對態度。

The political stance of the working class in this country has varied across the region.

這國家藍領階級的政治立場因地區而異。

❖ 常用搭配詞

adj. + stance

political, aggressive, moral, tough, critical, public, positive, neutral, negative, basic, conservative, ideological, different, changed, rigid, good, anti-abortion, firm, neutral, paternalistic, similar, uncompromising, independent, conciliatory, traditional, feminist, official, liberal, strong, theoretical, intransigent, educational, impartial, earlier, natural, belligerent, militant, opposite, pro-Iraqi, confrontational, robust, Soviet, competitive, initial, interventionist, general, Syrian, original, friendly, pragmatic, tougher, apologetic, correct, radical, strategic, threatening, professed, professional, skeptical, unified, passive, economic, normal, appreciative, moderate, corrective, proper, authoritarian.

v. + a + adj. + stance

adopt, take, maintain, have.

綜合整理

position	對某件事情的意見、看法、或判斷，尤其是政府、政黨、或權位人士的官方立場。後面介系詞常用on。另外還有其他意義，最常見的是姿勢，另外還表示處境、位置、方向、職位等，因此在語料庫中此字前面可能接的形容詞非常多，但其意義必需視上下文而定，例如official position就可能是官方立場或官職。
attitude	個人對某件事情的意見或感受，後面介系詞常用toward或to。attitude除了指對外在人事物的意見或感受（如skeptical attitude），也表示自身所抱持的處理態度及做法（如conservative attitude）。另外也表示前衛叛逆的服裝打扮和行為。
stance	公開表述的意見、立場，後面介系詞常用on或against。stance除了指對外在人事物的意見或感受（如skeptical stance），也表示自身所抱持的處理態度及做法（如conservative stance），前面出現的形容詞和attitude前面出現的形容詞有許多相同。另外也表示姿勢或位置。

Unit 72 立誓

StringNet語料庫出現次數

swear	pledge	vow
2146	1035	632

swear（vi./vt.）

❖ 常用句型

S + swear（to sombody）that + 子句
S + swear to + Vroot

❖ 例句

He was to be sworn in as President on May 20.
他會在5月20日宣誓就任總統。
The members who made the decision are sworn to secrecy.
做成這個決定的會員被要求發誓保密。
The boy said, “I didn’t steal the money. I swear”.
這男孩說：「我發誓我沒偷錢!」
The bridegroom swore to the bride that he would love her to the grave and beyond.
那位新郎對新娘發誓說會永遠愛她。

❖ 常用搭配詞

be sworn in as（adj.）+ n.

minister, president, council, governor, head, chancellor, commander, chairman.

swear + n.

allegiance, fealty, vengeance, fidelity, enemies, loyalty, oaths, obedience, revenge, devotion.

pledge（vt.）

❖ 常用句型

S + pledge something to something/somebody
S + pledge + to Vroot
S + pledge that + 子句
S + pledge oneself to（do）something

❖ 例句

He pledged $10,000 to the charity foundation in the fund-raising party.
他在那場募款餐會上認捐一萬元給那個慈善基金會。

The new mayor pledged to reduce unemployment rate.
新市長誓言要降低失業率。

The new members of the club are required to pledge their loyalty.
這俱樂部的新會員被要求發誓效忠這個俱樂部。

❖ 常用搭配詞

pledge one's + n.

support, loyalty, husband, commitment, allegiance, future, backing, sword, credit.

pledge to + v.

fight, continue, reduce, support, try, help, increase, take, keep, do, work, provide, end, give, investigate, abolish, maintain, cut, restore, make, put, buy, prevent, introduce, retain, stay, oppose, stop, stick, protect, resettle, save, raise, use, review, intensify, renew, brief, limit, freeze, build, vote, follow, recycle, lead, improve, adopt, promote.

vow（vt.）

❖ 常用句型

S + vow that + 子句

S + vow +（not）to Vroot

❖ 例句

He vowed never to return to his hometown.

他發誓永遠不再回到家鄉。

The nuns have vowed never to get married.

這些尼姑發誓永不結婚。

The worker vowed that it would never happen again.

那名工人發誓不會再犯。

❖ 常用搭配詞

vow never to + v.

return, have, get, play, sell, touch.

vow to + v.

fight, continue, carry, make, go, take, return, do, stay, keep, kill, stand, get, give, put, defend, remember, work, defy, stop, break, leave, attack, campaign, love, pursue, step, support, rescue, maintain, destroy, improve, repeal.

綜合整理

swear	發誓自己一定會做某件事情，也指公開的承諾，如法庭上的誓言（swear an oath to tell the truth）、員工的保密條款（be sworn to secrecy），以及宣誓就職等（be sworn in），swear to + Vroot的句型在語料庫中很少出現，比較常見swear that + 子句。在非正式的用法中也表示發誓某件事情的真實性。
pledge	正式或公開發誓自己一定會做某件事情，或使人保證做某件事情，在語料庫中常見pledge + to Vroot的句型。
vow	和promise相似。很嚴肅地向自己或別人發誓，也指信仰上對上帝或對教會的誓言，在語料庫中常見vow not + to Vroot和vow to Vroot的句型。

Unit 73 利益，利潤

StringNet語料庫出現次數

interest	benefit	profit	return	advantage	gain	margin
37054	15005	11211	10977	10058	3543	2592

interest（n.）

❖ 常用句型

It + be in one's （best） interest（s）（to do something）
It is in the（adj.）interest（s）（of someone）（to do something）/（+ that 子句）

❖ 例句

The judge decided that it was in the black boy's best interests to leave his white adopted parents and go back to his black biological mother.
法官判決為了這個黑人男童的最大益處，他應該離開他的白人養父母，歸回他的黑人生母。

It is in the national interest to join WTO.
加入世界衛生組織是出於國家利益。

The syndicate has obvious vested interests to protect.
這財團明顯要保護他們的既得利益。

He has your best interests at heart.
他很關心你的利益。

❖ 常用搭配詞

v. + one's interests

protect, represent, defend, pursue, safeguard, promote, sell, extend, know, see, perceived, press, have, serve, realize, develop, identify, suit, expand, assert, reflect, affect, disclose, advance, merge, share.

in the + adj. interests of

best, long-term, economic, long-run, strategic, common, true.

benefit（n.）

❖ 常用句型

S + be of benefit（to somebody）= S + be to the benefit of somebody

❖ 例句

The goal of the organization is to undertake projects of benefit to local communities.

這個組織的目的是從事對當地社區有益的計畫案。

It sounds encouraging that you can reap the benefits of exercise in 90 minutes a week.

你一周運動90分鐘就有獲益，聽起來滿鼓舞人心的。

The task of this committee is to evaluate local environmental protection projects in terms of costs and benefits.

這個委員會的任務是評估本地環保計畫案的成本和效益。

❖ 常用搭配詞

v. + the benefit

have, reap, get, enjoy, see, give, feel, provide, claim, lose, offer, obtain, appreciate, deny, achieve, outweigh, recognize, discover, extend, consider, share, want, maximize, realize, bring, take, spread, exceed, retain, reduce, assess, explain, extol, think, explore, secure, promote, increase, estimate, seek, demonstrate, discuss, show, emphasize, examine, outline, experience, pass, acquire, value.

adj. + benefit

economic, great, marginal, potential, full, financial, maximum, mutual, real, environmental, future, additional, major, significant, many, main, long-term, direct, extra, personal, tangible, public, obvious, private, added, positive, possible, considerable, net, substantial, practical, certain, enormous, external, total, commercial, immediate, medical, defined, general, lasting, perceived, clear, key, likely, following, common, immense, therapeutic, expected, contributory, psychological, educational, double, overall, taxable, various, political, ultimate, related, tremendous, statutory, universal, physical, tentative, increasing, actual, occupational, measurable, current, accrued, strategic, joint, sole, basic, claimed, human, gratuitous, spiritual, supposed, secondary, genuine, relative, sider, dubious, collective, specific, reduced, average, fiscal, preserved, large, resulting, visible, distinct, unjust, accelerated, intangible, inestimable, aesthetic, definite, equal, comprehensive, relevant, guaranteed, attractive, associated, proven, limited, global, desirable, premium, accompanying, consequent, technical, modest, exclusive, recreational, hidden, anticipated, incalculable, multiple, mobile, adequate, individual, extended, pecuniary, incidental, initial, low, whorthwhile.

profit（n.）

❖ 常用句型

S + make/turn + a（adj.）profit
at a + adj. + profit

❖ 例句

To the end of November the company made a profit of $1.2million — 5 per cent up on the same period last year.
到了十一月底這家公司獲利120萬美元，比去年同期多了百分之五。
They sold their farm at a huge profit.
他們賣掉農場，得到一大筆利潤。
Businesses are making a desperate attempt to cut costs and boost profits due to the long-lasting depression.
因為長久以來的不景氣，各行各業想盡辦法降低成本和提高利潤。
The general director wants you to turn in the profit and loss account for this year.
總經理要你交給他今年的損益表。

❖ 常用搭配詞

adj. + profit

net, pre-tax, gross, taxable, all, annual, good, high, increased, small, potential, large, interim, corporate, private, high, lower, short-term, excess, healthy, future, maximum, distributable, expected, quick, overall, substantial, total, retained, consolidated, fat, little, lost, modest, handsome, enormous, strong, attributable, personal, reasonable, reported, excessive, vast, unrealized, current, financial, considerable, massive, relevant, commercial, actual, normal, average, underlying, declining, easy, additional, tidy, worldwide, secret, combined, budgeted, poor, useful, illegal, illicit, pure, depressed, surplus, sizeable, hefty, immediate, speculative, undrawn, decent, individual, solid, aggregate, accumulated, assessable, excellent, realized, ultimate, agreed, fair, enhanced, dramatic, impending, monetary, dwindling, negative, anticipated, decreasing, optimal, steady.

v. + profit

make, maximize, increase, generate, boost, earn, push, cut, take, calculate, maintain, erode, expect, produce, achieve, share, see, show, report, have, reduce, squeeze, raise, shift, restore, forget, create, record.

return（n.）

❖ 常用句型

return on/from something

❖ 例句

The shareholders wanted to be assured of a good return on their money.
股東們希望能確保他們投資的錢能有利潤。
The average rate of return is 5%.
平均回報率是百分之五。

❖ 常用搭配詞

a + adj. return

good, quick, reasonable, rapid, adequate, fair, poor, financial, positive, high, speedy, gradual, satisfactory, net, swift, immediate, expected, general, attractive, possible, small, total, lucrative, decent, double, substantial, eventual, partial, easy, spectacular, safe, instant, abnormal, proper, phased, full, excellent, complete, minimum, diminishing, worrying, direct, likely, economic, short-term, gross, slight, riskless, rare, tax-free, end-of-year, huge, acceptable, temporary, permanent, actual, average.

return on + n.

capital, investment, assets, equity, sales, money, savings, deposits, shares, treasury.

v. +（det.）good return on

get, provide, give, produce.

advantage（n.）

❖ 常用句型

It + be + to somebody's advantage to do something
something + be/work to somebody's advantage
Somebody + be at an advantage

❖ 例句

Living in Taipei, where there are more job opportunities, is to your advantage.
住在台北對你有利，因為工作機會比較多。
It is to your advantage to start as early as possible.
愈早開始對你愈有利。
Good-looking people seem to be at an advantage when applying for jobs.
外表好看的人在求職時似乎較有優勢。

❖ 常用搭配詞

adj. + advantage

full, great, competitive, best, added, own, unfair, comparative, big, main, major, distinct, political, additional, obvious, pecuniary, significant, considerable, real, maximum, economic, clear, electoral, personal, little, financial, military, commercial, enormous, strategic, immediate, huge, principal, potential, better, tactical, practical, psychological, relative, tremendous, temporary, possible, positive, good, slight, long-term, territorial, small, selective, general, decided, initial, apparent, double, chief, definite, inestimable, dubious, technological, undue, prime, biological, human, informational, instant, equal, social, natural, extra, theoretical, substantial, twofold, fundamental, kinetic, administrative, private, collective, inbuilt, inherent, automatic, sexual, one-stroke.

gain（n.）

❖ 常用句型

S + V + adj. + gain
gain on/from + N/Ving

❖ 例句

The political party made significant gains during the campaign.
這個政黨在這次活動中大有斬獲。

$1.3m gains from the sale of stock and $320,000 gains from payment of debt
股票銷售所得130萬以及債務償付所得32萬元。

capital gains tax on share market dealing
股票市場交易的資本利得稅。

❖ 常用搭配詞

adj. + gain（s）

net, financial, personal chargeable, potential, short-term, recognized, significant, economic, capital, substantial, ill-gotten, real, own, major, small, unrealized, commercial, private, closed-loop, current, exceptional, large, extraordinary, expected, open-loop, modest, early, monetary, immediate, considerable, possible, strong, pre-tax, great, solid, overall, environmental, military, political, low, marginal, taxable, pecuniary, individual, electoral, enormous, maximum, general, sharp, huge, spectacular, automatic, likely, projected, con-recurring, short-run, obvious, temporary, average, limited, unfair, strategic, entire, qualitative, direct, relative, future, ultimate, instant, double-digit, mutual, large-scale, additional, positive, initial.

v. + adj. gain

make, bring, offer, have, generate, enjoy, represent, sacrifice, achieve, show.

margin（n.）

❖ 例句

profit margin利潤率

Many shoe factories were shut down because the margins were low.

許多鞋廠因為利潤太低而關閉。

❖ 常用搭配詞

n. + margin

profit, safety, variation, solvency, trading, percent, cost, rate, fluctuation, marketing.

adj. + margin

gross, initial, narrow, large, low, high, pre-tax, considerable, huge, small, significant, better, discounted, substantial, generous, increasing, reasonable, decent, clear, overall, political, adequate, profitable.

綜合整理

interest	泛指對某人或某事有好處的利益（一般用複數），如既得利益（vested interest）。也表示借貸的利息（不可數）。此字主要的意義是興趣或趣味，語料庫中出現次數多，但不都是表示利益的意思。
benefit	得到益處，尤其指使人得到某方面的改善或幫助，如健康、教育學習、或經濟上的益處等。在語料庫中大表示政府發放的救濟金、福利金、或津貼等補助，如失業補助（unemployment benefit）。
profit	買賣的利潤，扣掉成本後的贏利，如淨利潤（net profit）。
return	和profit相似，尤指個人投資的獲利（return on one's investment）。
advantage	對某人有利的事物，有利的條件或因素。
gain	藉著努力或計劃而獲得的好處、利益、或改進。
margin	賣掉某商品的價值扣除買進或生產該商品的花費所得的利潤，常出現在專有商業術語。

Unit 74 裂痕，裂縫

StringNet語料庫出現次數

breach	crack	fracture	fissure	crevice	cleft
3439	1775	581	186	164	121

breach（n.）

❖ 例句

John doesn’t want to cause a breach with his neighbor.
John 不想和鄰居關係破裂。
There has been a breach of security in the ocean guard.
這裡的海防有漏洞。

❖ 常用搭配詞

v. + breach of

prevent, cause, restrain, provoke, involve, deny, induce, anticipate, admit.

adj. + breach

any, serious, alleged, fundamental, such, clear, anticipatory, grave, possible, major, minor, actual, technical, particular, gross, substantial, future, threatened, open, initial, trivial, subsequent, mere, improper, final, significant, imminent, relevant, potential, real, admitted, past, irremediable, widespread, distinct, widening, complete, obvious, persistent, occasional, ordinary.

breach in + n.

wall, relationships, cliffs, intima, barrier, integrity, embankment.

crack（n.）

❖ 例句

There is a long, thin crack in the screen of his smart phone.
他的智慧型手機螢幕有一條細長的裂痕。
She opened the door a crack to see who was there.
她把門開一點縫隙看看誰在那裏。

❖ 常用搭配詞

n. + crack

hairline, corner, surface, exit, curving, fingertip.

adj. + crack

tiny, thin, big, small, wide, steep, horizontal, faint, huge, eroded, gaping, narrow.

fracture（n.）

❖ 例句

He has a stress fracture in his right knee.
他的右膝蓋有壓力性骨折。

❖ 常用搭配詞

n. + fracture

stress, skull, hairline, hip, compound, fatigue, leg, rock, bone, rib, cheekbone.

fracture of the + n.

skull, leg, cheekbone, shin, spine, jaw, arm, tibia.

fissure（n.）

❖ 例句

The photograph shows a kilometer-long fissure in the earth caused by an earthquake.

這張照片顯示地震後造成地面長度約一公里的裂縫。

❖ 常用搭配詞

fissure in the + n.

rock, limestone, cone, anthill, surface, canyon, roof, earth, cliff.

adj. + fissure

new, narrow, numerous, great, volcanic, kilometer-long.

crevice（n.）

❖ 例句

Rock doves nest in a rock crevice or cave ledge.
野鴿在岩石裂縫或洞穴裡的岩架築巢。

❖ 常用搭配詞

n. + crevice
rock, bark.

cleft（n.）

❖ 例句

The fugitive hid in a cleft in the rocks for several days.
這逃犯在一堆岩石中的一個岩縫躲了幾天。

❖ 常用搭配詞

cleft in the + n.
rock, mountain, flesh, center, earth, cliff.

adj. + cleft
deep, synaptic, dark, narrow, conspicuous, black, slippery.

綜合整理

breach	最常見的意義是違反法律、協議，或侵犯他人權利。表示破裂時有二個意義：（1）保護牆或堤防的缺口；（2）二人關係的破裂，嫌隙。因為有多種意義，所以在語料庫中出現次數衆多。
crack	可以指二個物體之間，或一個物體的二部分之間斷裂的狹窄裂縫，或沒有裂開的細長裂痕。此字另有其他多種意義。
fracture	大多用來表示骨折（斷裂或只有裂痕），但也可以指其他硬物的裂縫。
fissure	很深的裂縫，尤其在地表或岩石，例如地震造成地面的裂縫。
crevice	表面狹窄的裂縫，尤其是岩石，例如小動物藏身的岩縫。
cleft	自然形成的裂縫，尤其是在岩石或地表，也用來表示兔唇。

補充：另外gap表示裂縫時指一個物件因為缺了某個小部分而造成缺口，如籬笆的缺口。也指二物之間的間隔，及二山之間的峽谷。雖然在語料庫中出現次數比其他單字高，但是大部分是其他意義，所以在此不深入探討。

Unit 75 裂開

StringNet語料庫出現次數

crack	breach	fracture
1475	611	152

crack（vi./vt.）

❖ 常用句型

S + crack（+O）

❖ 例句

Suddenly the glass of the table cracked after he put the cup of boiling water on it.
他把那杯滾燙的水放在桌上後桌子的玻璃突然裂開。

❖ 常用搭配詞

crack +（det.）n.
nut, egg, bone, shell, glass, bottle, toe, car, rib.

the + n. crack
glass, ice, earth, windscreen.

breach（vt.）

❖ 常用句型

S + breach + O

❖ 例句

The artillery breached the wall of the castle.
大砲把城牆炸開一個洞。

❖ 常用搭配詞

breach the + n.
walls, injunction, surface, trust.

fracture（vi./vt.）

❖ 常用句型

S + fracture +（+O）

❖ 例句

The fugitive died from falling down from the balcony and fracturing his skull.
那位逃犯的死因是從陽台摔落造成頭骨破裂。

❖ 常用搭配詞

fracture one's + n.

skull, eye, jaw, hip, kneecap, spine, back.

綜合整理

crack	表示打破某物，使產生線狀裂痕或裂開成塊狀。另有其他多種意義。
breach	指使保護牆出現破洞。另外也指違約或違法。
fracture	破裂或斷裂，通常指骨折，也指團體因為意見不合而分裂。

Unit 76 聯絡，聯繫

StringNet語料庫出現次數

reach	contact	liaise
22346	5406	297

reach（vt.）

❖ 常用句型

S + reach + 人 at/ on + 電話號碼

❖ 例句

You may reach her on her cell phone.
你可以打她的手機和她連絡。
You may reach me at/ on 321-3211.
你可以打電話到321-3211找我。

❖ 常用搭配詞

reach + n.（人）
her, us, me, you, George, Simon, Ruth, Mr., Ms.

contact（vt.）

❖ 常用句型

S + contact + 人 at/ on + 電話號碼

❖ 例句

Anyone interested should contact Ms. Lin on 0730 892087.
有興趣的人請打0730 892087聯絡林小姐。

❖ 常用搭配詞

contact the（n）+ n.
police, office, council, officer, section, administrator, liaison, station, department, unit, secretary.

liaise（vi.）

❖ 常用句型

S + liaise + with/ between + N

❖ 例句

Homes for unmarried mothers may liaise with the adoption agency to find suitable families for babies to be adopted.
未婚媽媽之家也會和認養機構聯繫，以幫助供人認養的嬰兒找到適當的家庭。

❖ 常用搭配詞

liaise with +（det.）n.

department, group, party, caterers, police, media, agency, society, priest, committee, office, service, center.

綜合整理

reach	設法和某人講話或打電話給某人。雖然在語料庫中出現次數多，但是絕大多數是其他意義。電話號碼前面美加地區較常用at，英國和澳洲等地區則習慣用on。
contact	寫信或打電話給某人。
liaise	指和不同部門或機構的人交換資訊，以使工作順利完成，後面時常接with + 機構名稱。

Unit 77 練習，演練

StringNet語料庫出現次數

practice	exercise	drill
21334	7715	1013

practice（n.）

❖ 例句

She volunteered to play the organ at choir practice.
她自願在詩班練習時彈風琴。

❖ 常用搭配詞

n. + practice

class, work, teaching, group, shool, choir, language.

exercise（n.）

❖ 例句

Balancing exercise is essential for a ballet student.
平衡練習對學芭蕾舞的學生很重要。

❖ 常用搭配詞

n. + exercise

consultation, training, breathing, balancing, marketing, relaxation, assessment, evaluation, research, paper, group, school, waist, problem-solving, warm-up, writing, modeling, simulation, morning, comprehension, pilot, team, role-playing, classroom, translation, muscle, finger.

adj. + exercise

this, military, regular, physical, whole, aerobic, practical, vigorous, similar, useful, gentle, proper, mental, joint, strenuous, written, intellectual, technical, spiritual, daily, stretching, pattern-matching, listening, mathematical, role-play, deep-breathing, intensive, indoor.

drill（n.）

❖ 例句

Nancy is tired of the daily grammar drill.
Nancy 對日復一日的文法練習感到厭煩。

❖ 常用搭配詞

n. + drill

pronunciation, fire, safety, evacuation, rifle, grammar, laboratory.

綜合整理

practice	相對於理論（theory），表示練習的行為或活動，如詩班練習（choir practice）。前面接形容詞時大多表示其他意義如常規、慣例、執業等。
exercise	指經過設計以協助精進技能的活動或程序，可以指書本的練習題目、軍事演練、或鍛鍊體力的體能活動，前面常接形容詞表示練習的種類（如deep-breathing exercise）或性質（proper exercise）。另有其他多種意義。
drill	當名詞時最常表示電鑽，表示練習時則是指包含重複性練習的訓練方法，如學生的發音練習（pronunciation drill）、軍隊的行進或武器練習（rifle drill）、或安全演習（fire drill）等。

Unit 78 臨時的，暫時的

StringNet語料庫出現次數

temporary	provisional	transitional	tentative
3775	907	721	560

temporary（adj.）

❖ 例句

The factory is recruiting 40 temporary workers.
這工廠在徵40名臨時工人。

❖ 常用搭配詞

temporary + n.

workers, accommodation, basis, jobs, measure, labor, exhibitions, traffic light, provisions, working, employment, home, nature, relief, suspension, loss, solution, reputation, contracts, phenomenon, respite, setback, closure, aberration, reprieve, halt, period, residents, use, arrangement, office, storage, buildings, blip, replacement, ceasefire, ban, repair, phase, truce, permission, refuge, condition, licence, membership, name, protection, blindness, position, effect, help, bridge, secretary, decline, depression.

provisional（adj.）

❖ 例句

A provisional government was formed after the civil war.
內戰結束後臨時政府成立。

❖ 常用搭配詞

provisional + n.

government, grant, licence, damages, figures, council, president, agreement, liquidator, committee, list, movement, date, results, nature, basis, executive, title, world, estimate, booking, view, repayments, collection, settlement, report, proposals, measure, recognition, approval, leadership, membership, data, code, treatment.

transitional（adj.）

❖ 例句

The transitional period was extended for negotiation between the union and the employer.
過渡期被延長，以利工會和雇主的談判。

❖ 常用搭配詞

transitional + n.

period, government, relief, arrangements, provisions, authority, phase, stage, probabilities, legislature, zone, forms, constitution, state, executive, style, parliament, administration, measures, coalition, assistance, cell, protection, process, grant, year, reduction, committee, group, benefit, change, season, cabinet, status, president, problems.

tentative（adj.）

❖ 例句

She took her first tentative steps toward stardom in Hollywood.
她在好萊塢初試啼聲，邁向星途。
Only tentative conclusions can be drawn from the experiment because the sample was very small.
由於這個實驗的樣本數很小，所以只能獲得試驗性的結論。

❖ 常用搭配詞

tentative + n.

steps, conclusions, smile, benefit, approach, date, start, suggestions, beginnings, way, moves, plans, diagnosis, belief, support, nature, identification, agreement, hypothesis, expression, commitment, exploration, manner, application, enquiries, supposition, experiments, signs, proposals, solution, speculation.

綜合整理

temporary	持續或被使用一段有限的時間，相對於永久（permanent）。後面名詞時常和工作、職員、建築物等有關。
provisional	正式用字。表示臨時的、未來會改變的，最常用於臨時政府（provisional government）。
transitional	過渡型的（如transitional government），指新政府尚未選舉產生之前的政府。後面名詞時常和政府或立法等有關。
tentative	暫時性的、試驗性的、尚未確定、之後可能會改變的。雖然意義和provisional相似，但是多了試驗性質的意味（如tentative steps），因此後面的名詞會有步驟（step）、行動（move）、實驗（experiment）等意義。另外也指沒信心的。

以上單字有許多相同的搭配詞，如license, government, arrangement, nature等，但是出現次數則不盡相同，例如臨時駕照最常出現的是provisional license，臨時政府最常用provisional government，臨時安排最常用transitional arrangements，而短暫的本質則最常用temporary nature。

Unit 79 吝嗇的，小氣的

StringNet語料庫出現次數

miserly	ungenerous	parsimonious	stingy
46	36	35	34

miserly（adj.）

❖ 例句

After her miserly grandfather died, she was surprised to know that he proved to be worth nearly 50 million dollars.
當她吝嗇的祖父過世後，她很驚訝地發現他的身價值將近五千萬元。

❖ 常用搭配詞

miserly + n.
people, attitude, character, contractor, man, great-uncle, hosts.

ungenerous（adj.）

❖ 例句

He regretted his earlier ungenerous thought.
他後悔先前心胸狹窄的想法。

❖ 常用搭配詞

ungenerous + n.

idea, thought, lover, feeling, intention, husband.

parsimonious（adj.）

❖ 例句

The government needed to be more parsimonious given the financial crisis.

由於財務的危機，政府必須更省吃儉用。

parsimonious + n.

government, levels, ministers.

stingy（adj.）

❖ 例句

The board of the company are very stingy when it comes to overheads.

這公司的董事會對於經常費用非常吝嗇。

❖ 常用搭配詞

stingy + n.

uncle, race, thing, gift.

綜合整理

miserly	不慷慨的，不喜歡花錢的，像守財奴般貪戀錢財而一毛不拔。另外也指少量的、微薄的。
ungenerous	心胸狹窄而不願意付出、分享、或饒恕的。另外表示不仁慈的。
parsimonious	正式用字，指極端、不願意花錢、過於儉省的。另外表示簡約的（如parsimonious explanation）。
stingy	非正式用字。不慷慨的，尤其是在金錢上。

補充：cheap和mean二字也有吝嗇的意思，cheap是美式口語用字，表示小氣不肯花錢的（例如He is too cheap to take a taxi. 他很小氣，不肯搭計程車），相當於英式用字mean。mean表示不願意花錢的或盡量少用某物的（例如They are mean with ham. 他們對於火腿吃得非常省），屬於英式英文用字，類似stingy和美式用字的cheap。這二個字在語料庫中出現次數很多，但是絕大多數都是其他意義，因此在此沒列出。

Unit 80 領域

StringNet語料庫出現次數

field	territory	domain
20321	4420	2156

field（n.）

❖ 例句

He is an expert in his field.
他在他的領域是專家。

❖ 常用搭配詞

the field of + n.

study, research, education, interest, knowledge, activity, science, business, work, art, employment, communication, production, endeavor, design, health, computer, engineering, language, justice, practice, energy, management, sociology, law, medicine, biology, economics, industry, nurse, trade, linguistics, architecture, sport, anthropology, theology, chemistry, music.

territory（n.）

❖ 例句

They have made a leap into new territory.
他們已經躍進新的領域。

❖ 常用搭配詞

adj. + territory

unknown, new, uncharted, unexplored, forbidden.

domain（n.）

❖ 例句

This issue is outside of the domain of international law.

這個議題已經超出國際法的領域。

❖ 常用搭配詞

the domain of + adj. + n.

social reform, social experience, social deixis, disciplinary research, disciplinary enquiry, syntactic analysis, syntactic knowledge, applied linguistic, scientific pursuit, foreign politics, human rights, cultural form, everyday life, popular cinema, professional education, personal relations.

the domain of + n.

banking, pragmatics, discourse, language, sociolinguistics, science.

綜合整理

field	研究的主題或工作的活動範圍，後面常接有關學科或工作的名詞。
territory	特殊範圍的知識或經驗，如新的或熟悉的經驗。
domain	正式用字。知識、興趣或活動的領域，尤其是機構或個人長期從事的。另外也指領土。

Unit 81 魯莽

StringNet語料庫出現次數

reckless	impulsive	rash	foolhardy	impetuous
539	196	157	98	71

reckless（adj.）

❖ 例句

Tom's 18-year-old son was charged with causing death by reckless driving.
Tom的兒子被控危險駕駛致死。

❖ 常用搭配詞

reckless + n.

driving, manslaughter, disregard, abandon, behavior, drivers, killing, courage, step, haste, teenager, fool, vigilantes, endangerment, path, act, intent, way, form, spirit, fellow, manner, urgent, moment.

impulsive（adj.）

❖ 例句

"Look before you leap" is a maxim impulsive people fail to follow.
「三思而後行」是魯莽衝動的人無法遵行的座右銘。

❖ 常用搭配詞

impulsive + n.

waves, components, nature, gesture, overdoses, act, people, decision, reaction, behavior, man.

rash（adj.）

❖ 例句

When you go shopping, take your time and avoid rash purchases.
當你逛街購物時，要慢慢來以避免在一時衝動下買東西。

❖ 常用搭配詞

rash + n.

challenge, statements, move, decision, predictions, assault, things, brother, speculation.

foolhardy（adj.）

❖ 例句

It is foolhardy to jeopardise your career because of a tentative laboratory report.
如果你讓一個暫時性的實驗室報告危及你的事業，那就太不智了。

❖ 常用搭配詞

foolhardy + n.

pledge, reference, visitor.

foolhardy to + v.
go, believe, say.

impetuous（adj.）

❖ 例句

The movie actor was taught to curb his natural impetuous temper.
這位電影明星學會克制他天生衝動的脾氣。

❖ 常用搭配詞

impetuous + n.
decision, way, nature.

綜合整理

reckless	不擔心自己行為可能造成的危險後果，在語料庫中最常用在危險駕駛（reckless driving），可以形容人或事物。
impulsive	沒有事先考慮到可能造成的危險或問題，可以形容人或事物。
rash	輕率，沒有考慮自己的行為是明智之舉，可以形容人或事物。與foolish相似。
foolhardy	有勇無謀，冒沒必要的險。與reckless相似，可以形容人或事物。在語料庫出現次數少，時常用在 It/ Somebody be foolhardy to + Vroot 的句型。
impetuous	急躁而沒事先考慮周延，可以形容人或事物。與impulsive相似。

Unit 82 旅行

StringNet語料庫出現次數

tour	journey	trip	travel
6746	5364	5532	3909

tour（n.）

❖ 例句

She decided to make a walking tour through the island for tranquility.
她決定要徒步旅行整個島嶼以尋求心靈寧靜。

❖ 常用搭配詞

tour + n.

operators, bus, manager, party, event, match, guide, card, dates, company, van, itinerary, player, package, captain, organizer, leader, schedule, group, titles, director, doctor, selectors, bookings, band, canlendar, record, outings, members, regulations, visitors, career, scheme, club.

n. + tour

world, UK, package, lecture, coach, winter, study, walking, mystery, concert, sightseeing, factory, cycle, challenge, group, city, air, bus, golf, exhibition, bike, season, comeback, cycling, team, music, safari, farewell, holiday, election, missionary, bicycle, illumination, car, camping, discovery.

adj. + tour

European, guided, American, grand, national, circular, short, overseas, whistle-stop, recent, current, inclusive, international, brief, nationwide, speaking, regional, promotional, fact-finding, four-day, regular, local, extended, disastrous, underground, enjoyable, independent, individual, annual, self-guided, exhausting.

journey（n.）

❖ 例句

They made a detour on their homeward journey to visit their uncle in New York.
在他們回家的旅途中，他們繞道去探訪他們住在紐約的叔叔。
The journey from innocence to experience can be painful but worthwhile.
從天真無邪到人生體驗的心路歷程可能是痛苦卻值得的。

❖ 常用搭配詞

n. + journey

return, train, bus, car, coach, rail, boat, taxi, night, sea, plane, road, marathon, day, missionary, ferry, desert, school, Jerusalem, helicopter, life.

adj. + journey

long, short, outward, homeward, epic, safe, wasted, hazardous, whole, entire, difficult, spiritual, daily, inner, arduous, grueling, final, extra, perilous, tiring, tortuous, pleasant, local, exciting, overnight, overland, tedious, return, regular, inward, expensive, two-week, lonely, adventurous, four-hour, various, comfortable, recent, dark, fateful, early, emotional, international, uneventful, Indian, seamless, circuitious, mystical, circular, treacherous, hurried, transcendent, fruitless, creative.

trip（n）.

❖ 例句

They took a day trip to a theme park 20 kilometers away.
他們到一個距離20公里的主題公園一日遊。
Did he buy a one-way ticket or a round-trip ticket？
他是買單程票還是來回票？

❖ 常用搭配詞

n. + trip

day, shopping, boat, school, business, return, field, fishing, coach, ego, weekend, hunting, river, camping, sight-seeing, skiing, pleasure, holiday, world, family, study, rafting, canoe, night, winter, cycle, dream, walking, nostalgia, safari, space, railway, motor, helicopter, marathon.

adj. + trip

this, round, short, long, recent, good, whole, quick, bad, foreign, several, frequent, overseas, successful, occasional, special, free, regular, wasted, weekly, annual, round-the-world, forthcoming, entire, local, rare, three-day, fantastic, over-night, planned, exciting, French, backpacking, secret, extended, safe, one-way, memorable, fruitless, brief, hour-long, romantic, direct, enjoyable, disastrous.

travel（n.）

❖ 例句

His new job involves a lot of travel.
他的新工作必須時常旅行。

❖ 常用搭配詞

travel+ n.

agent, agency, arrangements, service, industry, insurance, company, expenses, costs, book, time, documents, trade, firm, office, sickness, guides, business, borchures, market, writer, restrictions, plan, policy, facilities, concessions, center, club, information, bag, tickets, voucher, experience, group, delays, patterns, photographer, bug, diary, organizer, operators, requiremets, program, destinations, management, alarm, ban, news, pack, warrant, gamazine, editor, law, accident, enterprise, regulations, posters.

adj. + travel

return, visa-free, safe, early, light, easy, constant, frequent, extra, additional, recent, lon-distance.

綜合整理

tour	休閒娛樂性質的旅遊，可能只到一個或數個地點，常用在觀光旅遊相關用語（如tour director領隊，tour guide導遊），也指演藝人員的巡迴表演，或參觀某機構單位的導覽（如factory tour）。
journey	長距離的行程，也就是從一處到另一處的時間，也指人蛻變成長的漫長辛苦過程。英式英文用字，相當於美式用字的trip。
trip	到某地參觀或拜訪的行程，可能是娛樂性質或特定目的（如hunting trip, fishing trip），距離可近可遠。相當於英式用字的journey。
travel	從某個地方到另一個或數個地方的旅行，通常是指到遠處，當複數時常指娛樂性質的旅遊。

tour比較偏重有人幫忙規劃行程的旅遊，如tour operator/ company主要工作是幫忙顧客設計及規劃行程，也包含帶隊前往及導覽等；journey 雖然相當美式用字的trip，但多半指長距離，甚至艱苦的旅程，前面常接負面意義的形容詞（如tortuous journey, tiring journey等）；trip強調旅行的行程（如one-way trip單行票，round trip來回票），通常只有一個目的地，也包含運動類（如rafting trip, skiing trip）等有特殊目的的旅行；而travel強調旅行的行動本身，如travel agency的主要工作是替顧客訂機票及訂旅館等，以使旅行順利完成。

Unit 83 旅程

StringNet語料庫出現次數

course	voyage	itinerary
55045	841	261

course（n.）

❖ 例句

The hijacker forced the pilot to change the course of the plane.
劫機犯強迫機師改變飛機的航線。

❖ 常用搭配詞

n. + course
collision, water, easter, obstacle.

voyage（n.）

❖ 例句

Captain James Cook set out on his celebrated voyages of discovery from this estuary.
庫克船長是從這個海口灣出發開始他聞名的發現之旅。

❖ 常用搭配詞

n. + voyage

sea, return, ocean, beagle, China, fantasy.

adj. + voyage

maiden, long, epic, transatlantic, scientific, great, final, outward, whole, hazardous, exploratory, proposed, two-week.

itinerary（n.）

❖ 例句

She wrote a detailed itinerary for her backpacking trip to Japan.
她為她去日本的背包旅行寫了詳細的旅行路線計畫。

❖ 常用搭配詞

adj. + itinerary

detailed, intellectual, personal, full, demanding, circular, suggested.

one's + itinerary

their, your, his, our, my, her.

綜合整理

course	船或飛機的既定行程方向。另有其他許多意義，因此在語料庫出現次數相當多。
voyage	船隻或太空載具的長程航行。也指發現新知識或新事物的過程（voyage of discovery）。
itinerary	旅行的計畫路線，包含數個目的地，由於大多是客製化或個人自己訂定，前面常接所有格。

Unit 84 旅客，遊客

StringNet語料庫出現次數

visitor	passenger	tourist	traveler
6846	4432	3451	2452

visitor（n.）

❖ 例句

She is a frequent visitor to the museum.
她經常來參觀這間博物館。
His name is not found in the visitor's book.
在訪客登記簿上沒有他的名字。

❖ 常用搭配詞

visitors' + n.

book, center, room, questions, findings, cars, association, lead, hopes, attention, viewing, affections.

v. + visitors

have, attract, allow, give, welcome, get, receive, take, expect, tell, provide, like, make, show, offer, discourage, draw, pay, bring, encourage, help, protect, admit, invite, ask, introduce, advise, greet.

adj. + visitor

regular, frequent, foreign, overseas, casual, disabled, lawful, British, new, distinguished, important, royal, unwelcome, unexpected, recent, international, first-time, occasional, rare, famous, human, unusual, constant, unwanted, modern, strange, grand, temporary, interested, potential, future, local, entertaining, voluntary, outside, would-be, illustrious, official, increasing, ordinary, uninvited, undersirable, prospective, individual, pasing, inquisitive, seasonal, unauthorized, celebrated, heavy, handicapped, yearly, unsuspecting, defenceless.

passenger（n.）

❖ 例句

Airbags are developed to protect drivers and passengers in car crashes.
安全氣囊的研發是為了在汽車受到撞擊時保護駕駛人和乘客。

❖ 常用搭配詞

passenger + n.

seat, transport, door, traffic, train, services, aircraft, numbers, cars, compartment, terminal, casualties, comfort, railway, business, figures, window, lifts, list, ferry, jet, flight, coaches, manager, journeys, cabin, survey, vehicles, station, revenue, safety, facilities, handling, planes, fare, growth, section, accommodation, receipts, communication, charter, booking, committee, tickets, saloons, capacity, satisfaction, loadings.

adj. + passenger

fellow, international, disabled, first-class, regular, fare-paying, single, scheduled, front-seat, seated, local, civilian, arriving, domestic, elderly, remaining, injured, would-be, existing, human, innocent, early, commercial, hapless, ordinary, mysterious, rich, long-distance, drunken, Chinese, regional, royal, potential, national, individual, unwanted, standby, approaching, surviving, standing, angry, stranded, daily, increasing.

n. + passenger

bus, seat, rail, foot, pillion, airline, car, woman, air, business, wheelchair, coach, train, ferry, VIP, aircraft, child, transfer, adult.

v. + passengers

carry, take, protect, give, transport, get, bring, drop, pull, show, allow, attract, enable, offer, separate, drive, serve.

tourist（n.）

❖ 例句

The two typhoon-tilted post mailboxes have been ranked as Taiwan's most popular tourist attraction this year.

這二個因颱風導致傾斜的郵筒在今年台灣的熱門觀光景點中名列第一。

❖ 常用搭配詞

tourist + n.

board, industry, information, office, attraction, trade, authority, season, traffic, map, center, path, class, potential, destination, bus, resort, area, spots, accommodation, route, guides, hotel, facilities, business, market, trap, shops, town, association, visitors, sights, revenue, development, arrivals, boats, sites, agency, literature, coaches, visas, trail, police, tax, activities, charter, signs, rate, itinerary, brochures, commission, beaches, award, organization, project.

v. + tourists

attract, do, show, take, warn, carry.

adj. + tourist

British, English, American, popular, foreign, major, German, local, Japanese, national, main, regional, Western, modern, fellow, international, visiting, usual, early, adventurous, middle-class, increased.

traveler（n.）

❖ 例句

With the rise of Money Cards and ATMs, travelers' checks are falling out of vogue.
隨著貨幣卡和提款機的普及，旅行支票已經不再流行。
The stranded travelers had to spend the night in the airport.
受困的旅客只得在機場過夜。

❖ 常用搭配詞

travelers' + n.

checks, tales, guide, club, association, joy, fare, descriptions, aid, site, choice, insurance, booking, handbook, wardrobe, account, camp, advice, request.

adj. + traveler

commercial, fellow, weary, independent, frequent, English, new-age, seasoned, early, intrepid, experienced, discerning, international, British, foreign, regular, disabled, French, single, traditional, uncommercial, local, adventurous, lost, unwary, tired, curious, keen, overseas, inveterate, passing, prospective, ancient, ordinary, domestic, avid, hardened, lonely, returning, future, uneasy, hapless, official, remaining, individual, stranded.

n. + traveler

business, time, rail, air, space, armchair, train, world, express, night, north-west, airline.

綜合整理

visitor	訪客，亦即去參觀某地方或拜訪某人的人。
passenter	乘客，亦即搭乘交通工具的人，駕駛人及工作人員除外。
tourist	觀光客，亦即以休閒目的去參觀某處的人。
traveler	旅客，亦即在旅行中的人，或經常旅行的人。

Unit 85 旅館，旅舍

StringNet語料庫出現次數

hotel	inn	hostel	tavern	motel	B & B
13196	1817	851	415	168	68

hotel（n.）

❖ 例句

Her father is the manager of a five-star hotel.
她父親是一家五星級飯店的經理。

❖ 常用搭配詞

hotel + n.

room, accommodation, industry, group, bar, bedroom, suite, license, staff, manager, guests, lobby, management, chain, restaurant, business, bills, receptionist, owner, foyer, facilities, services, billage, propretors, porter, entrance, lounge, descriptions, market, details, reception, bookings, register, complex, corridor, expenses, development, environment, brochure, ballroom, suites, premises, coupons, kitchen, charges, security, reservation, companies, clerk, guide, operator, offers, features, system, occupancy, project, shop.

adj. + hotel

grand, small, five-star, luxury, modern, international, new, large, best, imperial, friendly, good, top, local, royal, family-run, comfortable, British, cheap, nearby, restricted, big, luxurious, private, major, first-class, elegant, commercial, excellent, western, intercontinental, beautiful, finest, leading, individual, attractive, delightful, exclusive, famous, pleasant, expensive, existing, splendid, oriental, prestigious, medium-sized, traditional, welcoming, independent, refurbished, selected, charming.

inn（n.）

❖ 例句

The Holiday Inn is one of the world's largest hotel chains.
假日飯店是全球最大的連鎖飯店之一。

❖ 常用搭配詞

n. + inn

Holiday, Coaching, Country, Swan, Hospitality.（以上皆是旅館名稱）

adj. + inn

new, old, blue, local, little, small, nearby, sizable, licensed, tiny, thatched, lighted, charming, early.

hostel（n.）

❖ 例句

They cut down on their travel expenses by staying at a youth hostel.
他們在青年旅館過夜以降低旅行開銷。

❖ 常用搭配詞

n. + hostel

youth, bail, army, probation, student, worker, refugee, community, staff, college, alcohol, hospital.

adj. + hostel

council-run, nearby, short-stay.

tavern（n.）

❖ 例句

The local tavern is a resting place for mine workers.
這家本地的小酒館是礦工們的休息處。

❖ 常用搭配詞

n. + tavern

Lion, Market, Hope & Anchor, Railway, Horse.（以上皆是旅館名稱）

adj. + tavern

local, small, dingy, refurbished, crowded, nearby.

motel（n.）

❖ 例句

His car was found in some motel parking lot.
他的車子被發現停在一家汽車旅館的停車場。

❖ 常用搭配詞

n. + motel
Katz, California, Budget.（以上皆是旅館名稱）

adj. + motel
two-year-old, large, comparable, garishly-lit.

B&B（NP）

❖ 例句

He is running a B&B in this village.
他在這個村子經營一家民宿。

❖ 常用搭配詞

n. + B&B
（seven）nights.

adj. + B&B
local.

綜合整理

hotel	規模較大的旅館，提供飲食，較高級的有游泳池、餐廳、會議室等設施。
inn	提供飲食的小旅館，通常在鄉村地區或在高速公路旁。在英式英文中指酒吧，有些飯店和酒吧的名字喜歡包含此字。
hostel	吃住都很廉價的旅館，通常是為青年背包客而設（如youth hostel），多人睡在同一間，床鋪是雙層床，共用衛浴設備、交誼廳、和廚房等，也有單人房。
tavern	英式英文老式用字，指提供住宿的酒吧，相當於inn。
motel	汽車旅館，通常在高速公路旁，可以把車子停在房間外面，價位通常比hotel低。
B & B	Bed and Breakfast，私人民宿，提供住宿和早餐，房間數目不多，通常在十間以下。

Unit 86 歌曲

StringNet語料庫出現次數

song	hymn
6752	672

song (n.)

❖ 例句

Many young people are interested in pop songs.
許多年輕人對流行歌曲很有興趣。

❖ 常用搭配詞

n. + song

love, folk, bird, Eurovision, hit, worship, theme, swan, title, torch, siren, Beatles, solo, Christmas, rock, opening, protest, chaffinch.

adj. + song

new, pop, popular, old, good, favorite, traditional, German, lovely, particular, beautiful, bawdy, famous, early, normal, simple, religious, marching, secular, polyphonic, gaelic, music-hall, sad, national, actual, bubbling, trilling, complex, comic, final, individual, divine, choral, distinct, tuneful, raucous, domestic, epic, strophic, romantic, aerial, thoughtful, rousing, spiritual, full, elaborate, brilliant, melodious, live, plantive, native, ritual, contemporary, bright, local, international, distinctive, anti-war, political, wild, bourgeios, big, catchy, emotional, courtly, odd, pathetic, commercial, published, ravishing, made-up, monophonic, varied, sacred, operatic, liquid.

hymn（n.）

❖ 例句

He likes to sing hymns even though he is not a Christian.
雖然他不是基督徒，他還是很喜歡唱讚美詩。

❖ 常用搭配詞

hymn + n.
book, writer, society, tune.

adj. + hymn
new, favorite, traditional, Lutheran, Methodist, modern, old, final, baptist, English, rousing, strange, familiar, best-known, homeric, lively, congregational, short.

n. + hymn
church, easter, opening, organ, morning.

綜合整理

song	泛指一般歌曲，包含動物如鳥類等發出的音樂。
hymn	教會讚美上帝的讚美詩。
補充：另外carol或Christmas carol指的是聖誕歌曲。	

Unit 87 各種的，各式各樣的

StringNet語料庫出現次數

various	diverse	varied	heterogeneous	assorted	sundry
15277	1310	1295	277	254	182

various（adj.）

❖ 例句

This community college offers courses of various kinds for senior citizens.
這間社區大學為銀髮族提供各式各樣的課程。

❖ 常用搭配詞

various + n.

ways, forms, kinds, parts, types, aspects, stages, reasons, times, groups, points, levels, methods, sources, people, factors, elements, sizes, countries, options, places, members, parties, areas, locaitons, sorts, combinations, activities, branches, degrees, items, government, functions, companies, theories, species, possibilities, measures, fields, techniques, ages, shades, schools, strategies, events, problems, positions, roles, jobs, languages, styles, changes, versions, media, directions, courses, churches.

diverse（adj.）

❖ 例句

The large class consists of students from a diverse range of backgrounds.
這個大班級包含來自不同背景的學生。
The shantytown was large and ethnically diverse.
那個貧名窟面積很大且包含各種不同種族的人。

❖ 常用搭配詞

diverse + n.

range, ways, interests, forms, group, cultures, needs, types, elements, population, activities, backgrounds, kinds, influences, interpretaions, roles, areas, nature, parts, collection, views, society, array, fields, country, patterns, skills, numbers, topics, locations, subjects, enterprises, phenomena, origins, products, flora, applications, experiences, opinions, aspects, styles, talents.

varied（adj.）

❖ 例句

This restaurant offers a varied selection of snacks.
這家餐廳提供各式各樣的甜點。
People who travel are as varied as their journeys.
旅行的人，正如他們的旅程一樣，有各式各樣。

❖ 常用搭配詞

varied + n.

program, diet, selection, range, forms, career, group, collection, experience, menu, interests, responses, activities, picture, ways, choice, nature, work, scenery, needs, types, backgrounds, situaitons, life, walks, problems, skills, history, quality, experiences, contributions, sources, character, landscanpe, form, results, use, curriculum, society, array.

many and varied + n.

attractions, ways, reasons, aspects.

heterogeneous（adj.）

❖ 例句

The new President will face a heterogeneous range of problems in the country.

新總統將會面對國內各種不同的問題。

❖ 常用搭配詞

heterogeneous + n.

group, collection, systems, networks, nature, population, chemistry, mixture, reactions, computing, data, processes, computer, array, catalysts, enterprises, histories, muddle, set, nucleation, genre, tasks, expectations, increase, markets, DNA, catalysis, elements, structure.

adv. + heterogeneous

more, extremely, rather, socially, most, ethically, essentially.

assorted（adj.）

❖ 例句

She chose carefully from the assorted vegetables on the shelf.
她從架子上各種排列整齊的蔬菜中仔細挑選。

❖ 常用搭配詞

assorted + n.

ammunition, vehicles, sizes, color, vegetables, bits, friends, beads, shapes, members, plastic, biscuits, jewellery, colorways, shops, papers, aches, uses.

sundry（adj.）

❖ 例句

This store sells socks, umbrellas, hair clips, gloves, and other sundry items.
這家店販售襪子、雨傘、髮夾、手套、和其他各式各樣品項。

❖ 常用搭配詞

sundry + n.

items, expenses, creditors, bills, charges.

綜合整理

various	同一項目之下的不同種類，通常放在名詞之前。後面名詞可以是抽象或具體的人事物。
diverse	彼此非常不一樣，相異。強調多元、不同的（如diverse cultures多元的文化，ethnically diverse種族多元等）。
varied	包含許多林林總總、各式各樣不同的人事物。
heterogeneous	正式用字，內部成員或各部分性質互異不同的。
assorted	混合各種不同類型的。
sundry	正式用字，相當於various。只能放在名詞之前，除了片語all and sundry（每一個人，一視同仁）以外。

Unit 88 概念，想法

StringNet語料庫出現次數

idea	concept	notion
31867	8985	4503

idea（n.）

❖ 例句

I have no idea why they broke up.
我不知道他們為甚麼分手。

❖ 常用搭配詞

v. + some idea of

have, give, get, form, gain.

a adj. + idea

good, bad, better, new, clear, great, rough, nice, vague, brilliant, general, fair, wonderful, splendid, bright, lovely, similar, simple, single, silly, fine, basic, novel, strange, marvellous, false, sound, crazy, ridiculous, shrewd, stupid, reasonable, sensible, clever, fixed, central, firm, particular, mad, definite, revolutionary, terrible, big, neat, certain, terrific, precise, complex, grand, further, strong, super, vivid, foolish, logical, familiar, wild, modern, sudden, curious, funny, one-off, wizard, smart, unique, realistic, popular.

concept（n.）

❖ 例句

The concept of liberal education goes back to the Greeks.
通才教育的概念始於希臘人。

❖ 常用搭配詞

v. + the concept of

introduce, use, develop, understand, support, reject, abandon, grasp, extend, accept, have, include, embrace, apply, invent, consider, propose, know, discuss, examine, explain, fit.

adj. + concept

new, whole, basic, key, general, two, legal, original, very, abstract, central, difficult, simple, fundamental, traditional, important, particular, mathematical, theoretical, modern, religious, scientific, relevent, underlying, broader, strategic, related, elusive, novel, vague, Christian, psychological, British, Marxist, relative, economic, intellectual, useful, single, western, political, spatial, limited, alien, entire, interesting, historical, complex, familiar, overall, linguistic, alternative, essential, old, initial, similar, own, personal, precise, dominant, easy, certain, social, problematic, moral, main, unifying, latter, clear, specific, mental, existing, ambiguous, natural, independent, emerging, cultural, sophisticated, technical, evolutionary, contemporary, high-level, medical, universal.

notion（n.）

❖ 例句

The traditional notion of family is facing tremendous challenge.
傳統的家庭觀念正面臨巨大的挑戰。

❖ 常用搭配詞

v. + the notion of

reject, extend, use, introduce, consider, accept, introduce, support, attack, come, propose, quenstion, entertain, revive, espouse, popularize, explain, like, challenge, include, define, abhor, retain.

adj. + notion

very, whole, general, simple, romantic, traditional, vague, preconceived, accepted, new, conventional, basic, abstract, modern, popular, clear, fundamental, false, simplistic, two, similar, theoretical, older, strange, absurd, English, mistaken, religious, psychological, intuitive, key, wider, complex, scientific, present, perceived, particular, hazy, current, confused, widerspread, philosophical, ridiculous, objective, political, alternative, cultural, foolish, legal, conservative, central, prevalent, limited, strong, cherished, crazy, fanciful, interesting, better, related, inflated, restricted, common, fancy, contemporary, spurious, dangerous, relative, misguided, brilliant, dubious, commonsense, ludicrous, underlying, stereotyped, alien.

綜合整理

idea	個人突然想到的作法、計畫、或建議。也指對某件事情的了解或看法。
concept	對某件事情的內容或作法的觀點，尤其是較複雜的學科經過縝密思考而得的概念（例如invent/ propose/ introduce the concept），前面常出現接專門學科的形容詞（如scientific, mathematical, medical等）。
notion	看法、意見、或信念，常指傳統、眾人認可的觀念（例如conventional/ cultural/ commonsense notion）。

Unit 89 高傲的，驕傲的

StringNet語料庫出現次數

insolent	proud	vain	arrogant	haughty
4503	3113	818	619	110

insolent（adj.）

❖ 例句

Josh's teacher was offended by his insolent tone.
Josh的老師被他傲慢的語氣激怒。

❖ 常用搭配詞

insolent + n.

tone, question, appraisal, children, affair, groom, provocation, demand, query, stare, treatment, way, answer, smile, refusal, sister, expression.

proud（adj.）

❖ 例句

Helen is proud to be on the school team.
Helen 以能參加校隊為榮。
Jessica is too proud to ask her friends for help.
Jessica 的自尊心太強而不願向朋友求助。

❖ 常用搭配詞

proud + n.

boast, owner, man, dad, parents, record, people, history, eye, race, tradition, position, assertion, moment, smile, naiton, past, face, prelates.

vain（adj.）

❖ 例句

He thinks Nancy is a vain girl and thinking too much about her figure.
他覺得Nancy是愛慕虛榮的女孩且太注意自己的身材。

❖ 常用搭配詞

vain + n.

man, woman, pomp, boast, actress, girl, prince.

arrogant（adj.）

❖ 例句

Henry returned to his seat with an arrogant shrug of his shoulders.
Henry回到他的座位同時傲慢地聳聳肩。

❖ 常用搭配詞

arrogant + n.

man, face, bastard, swine, manner, assumption, behavior, stare, way, attitude, grin, duchess, bully, dismissal, tone, assertion, eyes, profile.

haughty（adj.）

❖ 例句

The boy in his new suit stalked around like a haughty prince.
這小男孩穿著新西裝昂首闊步像個高傲的王子。

❖ 常用搭配詞

haughty + n.

face, disdain, manner, prince, man, looks, tyrants.

綜合整理

insolent	魯莽，不尊敬人。
proud	較常指引以為傲，感到光榮（be proud of/ to），也指把自己看得過度重要或過度有才能，也可表示自尊心過強而不願意接受別人的幫助，負面意義在此比其他單字程度較低。
vain	自負，自以為自己很特別，因為自己有好的能力，地位，尤其是外貌，常用來指女性愛慕虛榮。另外較常表示徒勞白費的。
arrogant	魯莽無禮，認為自己比別人重要。
haughty	行為舉止傲慢，目中無人。

Unit 90 港口

StringNet語料庫出現次數

port	dock	pier	jetty	harbor
4708	1938	1098	240	74

port（n.）

❖ 例句

The first port of call of the visiting princess is an orphanage in the city.
王妃出訪的第一站是這個城市中的一家孤兒院。
Both Constantinople and Venice were cosmopolitan cities and thriving commercial ports between the sixth and fourteenth centuries.
君士坦丁堡和威尼斯在第六世紀到十四世紀期間都是國際都市以及繁榮的商港。

❖ 常用搭配詞

adj. + port

serial, parallel, first, British, next, commercial, major, small, new, other, French, old, important, last, main, southern, free, Mediterranean, busy, foreign, largest, national, island, prosperous, warm-water, thriving, ancient, final, principal, various, naval, modern, distant, historic, coastal, provincial, vital, coal-exporting, local, small, military, bustling, native.

port + n.

authority, sunlight, Elizabeth, Glasgow, facilities, side, meadow, wing, mill, area, town, land, vila, transport, city, headland, operations, employers, operators, workers, activities, quarter, industry, services, dues, manager, traffic, development, house, business, police, system, tax, agent, council, complex, captain, hills, company, regiment, security.

dock（n.）

❖ 例句

The inhabitants near the docks were poor dock laborers.
住在碼頭附近的居民是貧窮的碼頭工人。

❖ 常用搭配詞

adj. + dock

dry, national, imperial, new, wet, old, large, upper, mooring, suitable.

dock + n.

company, commision, strike, workers, area, gates, laborers, facilities, leaf, identification, basin, system, ward, wall, estate, cranes, development, rail, office, complex, posts, side, assembly, yard, act, railway, duty, terminal, park, work, dues, engineering, mills, warehouse, forman.

pier（n.）

❖ 例句

On their return trip they paid a visit to the Brighton Pier.
他們在回程中去參觀了布萊頓碼頭。

❖ 常用搭配詞

n. + pier

Wigan, Palace, North, Wwest, Westminster, Navy, stone, Greenwich, railway, seaside, boat, iron.

jetty（n.）

❖ 例句

They bought a vila beside the lake with a private jetty.
他們買了一棟有私人棧橋的湖邊別墅。

❖ 常用搭配詞

adj. + jetty

wooden, private, new, small.

n. + jetty

stone, rock, ferry.

harbor（n.）

❖ 例句

The attack on Pearl Harbor led to the United States' entry into World War II.
珍珠港攻擊事件造成美國加入第二次世界大戰。

❖ 常用搭配詞

adj. + harbor
Little, post-Pearl.

n. + harbor
Pearl, Cold spring, Air, Bar.

綜合整理

port	輪船可以停泊及上下貨的地方，也可以指港口城市，所以範圍比harbor和dock大。Port of call = 沿途停靠的港口，衍伸為旅途的一站。Port當名詞有多種意義，所以在語料庫出現次數多，另外也當動詞或形容詞表示其他多種意義。
dock	船塢，碼頭，指port的一部分，供船隻上下貨及修理的地方。
pier	伸向海中的凸式碼頭，供船隻停靠或行人行走，下面通常有粗重的石柱、木柱、或鐵柱支撐，因此也可以用來指這類墩柱。在語料庫中大多用來表示墩柱，尤其是前面接形容詞時（例如four piers, concrete piers, wooden piers）等，因此在此不逐一列出。前面接名詞時大多是碼頭名稱（例如Brighton Pier, Navy Pier等）。在語料庫中後面接名詞時大多是姓氏，因為Piers是人名，因此在此不逐一列出。
jetty	伸向海中供人員上下船隻的棧橋或防波堤，與pier相似，但是不表示墩柱。後面不常接名詞，前面接名詞時表示材料（例如stone jetty和rock jetty）。
harbor	靠近陸地、風平浪靜、供船隻安全停泊的港灣或海港。語料庫中的資料幾乎均是珍珠港和其他港口名稱（例如Little Harbor 58, Sheraton Inner Harbor Hotel等），因此在此不逐一列出。

Unit 91 攻擊

StringNet語料庫出現次數

attack	assault
10585	2543

attack（n.）

❖ 例句

At least 29 people have been killed in the suicide attack in a crowded park in Iraq.
在這起發生在伊拉克一個人潮眾多的公園的自殺式攻擊事件中至少有29人喪生。

❖ 常用搭配詞

adj. + attack

unprovoked, first, personal, nuclear, direct, fierce, vicious, strong, severe, scathing, second, latest, major, violent, frontal, German, new, sudden, further, military, savage, two-pronged, French, brutal, chemical, verbal, serious, sexual, acute, full-scale, frenzied, armed, stinging, fungal, bad, Soviet, physical, massive, political, possible, similar, radical, better, initial, veiled, vitriolic, all-out, asthmatic, alleged, determined, aerial, recent, blistering, successful, final, immediate, motiveless, last, horrific, main, primary, devastating, real, racial, appalling, powerful, subsequent, car-bomb, impenidng, unprecedented, outspoken, deliberate, co-ordinated, allied, withering, continuous, random, scurrilous, external, viral, legal, mild, unexpected, retaliatory, suicidal, fatal, murderous, united, effective, furious, disguised, vocal, pre-emptive, abortive, despicable.

n. + attack

heart, bomb, arson, air, terrorist, surprise, panic, knife, sex, mortar, asthma, gun, counter, missile, rocket, ground, pace, revenge, gas, insect, enemy, acid, gurerrilla, anxiety, rebel, gang, daylight, rouge, army, street, collateral, virus, submarine, rape, land, jail, spirit, migraine.

v. + an attack

launch, have, suffer, mount, deter, follow, lead, plan, include, make, prepare, investigate, prevent, expect, trigger, relieve, involve, provoke, block, make, experience.

assault（n.）

❖ 例句

He is charged with rape and indecent assault.
他被控強暴及猥褻。

❖ 常用搭配詞

adj. + assault

sexual, indecent, common, physical, serious, frontal, alleged, direct, final, brutal, amphibious, violent, aggravated, vicious, verbal, major, military, first, successful, actual, initial, main, attempted, criminal, domestic, real, racial, constant, massive, new, full-scale, marine, technical, recent, homosexual, powerful, Japanese, repeated, systematic, monir, last, drunken, personal, murderous, right-wing, consensual, aggressive, deliberate.

n. + assault

army, sex, air, ground, parachute, knife, square, pop, monetarist, rebel, enemy, troop.

v. + an assault

launch, commit, constitute, mount, delay, bring, co-ordinate, involve, plan.

綜合整理

attack	使用暴力蓄意攻擊人或者某個地方，或是在戰爭以武器中攻擊敵人，前面時常接名詞表示各種戰爭工具（例如missile attack, acid attack）、戰爭位置（例如land attack, air attack），或接形容詞描述戰爭的性質（例如devastating attack, unprecedented attack）。另外也指言語的攻擊或者生理及心理疾病的發生。
assault	犯罪學用字，表示對個人人體的攻擊。雖然也表示在戰爭中攻擊敵區，但是不像attack那麼頻繁用在戰爭相關搭配詞。和attack一樣可以表示言語攻擊，但是不用在疾病的攻擊。

索引

英語辭彙不NG
——StringNet教你使用英文同義字（II）

作　　者 / 李路得
責任編輯 / 杜國維
圖文排版 / 賴英珍
封面設計 / 蔡瑋筠

出版策劃 / 秀威經典
發 行 人 / 宋政坤
法律顧問 / 毛國樑　律師
印製發行 / 秀威資訊科技股份有限公司
114台北市內湖區瑞光路76巷65號1樓
電話：+886-2-2796-3638　傳真：+886-2-2796-1377
http://www.showwe.com.tw
劃撥帳號 / 19563868　戶名：秀威資訊科技股份有限公司
讀者服務信箱：service@showwe.com.tw
展售門市 / 國家書店（松江門市）
104台北市中山區松江路209號1樓
電話：+886-2-2518-0207　傳真：+886-2-2518-0778
網路訂購 / 秀威網路書店：http://www.bodbooks.com.tw
國家網路書店：http://www.govbooks.com.tw

2016年12月　BOD一版
定價：600元

國家圖書館出版品預行編目

英語辭彙不NG : StringNet教你使用英文同義字.
(II) / 李路得著. -- 一版. -- 臺北市 : 秀威經典,
2016.12
面； 公分. -- (學語言 ; PD0049)
BOD版
ISBN 978-986-93753-9-9(平裝)

1. 英語 2. 同義詞 3. 詞彙

805.124 105020961

讀者回函卡

感謝您購買本書，為提升服務品質，請填妥以下資料，將讀者回函卡直接寄回或傳真本公司，收到您的寶貴意見後，我們會收藏記錄及檢討，謝謝！

如您需要了解本公司最新出版書目、購書優惠或企劃活動，歡迎您上網查詢或下載相關資料：http:// www.showwe.com.tw

您購買的書名：________________________________

出生日期：________年________月________日

學歷：□高中（含）以下　□大專　□研究所（含）以上

職業：□製造業　□金融業　□資訊業　□軍警　□傳播業　□自由業

□服務業　□公務員　□教職　□學生　□家管　□其它____

購書地點：□網路書店　□實體書店　□書展　□郵購　□贈閱　□其他

您從何得知本書的消息？

□網路書店　□實體書店　□網路搜尋　□電子報　□書訊　□雜誌

□傳播媒體　□親友推薦　□網站推薦　□部落格　□其他________

您對本書的評價：（請填代號　1.非常滿意　2.滿意　3.尚可　4.再改進）

封面設計____　版面編排____　內容____　文／譯筆____　價格____

讀完書後您覺得：

□很有收穫　□有收穫　□收穫不多　□沒收穫

對我們的建議：________________________________

____

____

____

請貼
郵票

11466
台北市內湖區瑞光路 76 巷 65 號 1 樓
秀威資訊科技股份有限公司 收
BOD 數位出版事業部

（請沿線對折寄回，謝謝！）

姓　　名：＿＿＿＿＿＿＿＿　年齡：＿＿＿＿　性別：□女　□男

郵遞區號：□□□□□

地　　址：＿＿＿＿＿＿＿＿＿＿＿＿＿＿＿＿

聯絡電話：(日)＿＿＿＿＿＿＿＿(夜)＿＿＿＿＿＿＿＿

E-mail：＿＿＿＿＿＿＿＿＿＿＿＿＿＿＿＿